The Young Wagoner

Surviving Braddock's Defeat 1755

R. Greg Lau

NEWMAN SPRINGS PUBLISHING
320 Broad Street
Red Bank, NJ 07701

First originally published by Newman Springs Publishing 2020

ISBN 978-1-64801-955-5 (Paperback)
ISBN 978-1-64801-956-2 (Digital)

Printed in the United States of America

This book is dedicated to my wonderful wife, Martha,
and the family she loves so much.

"I hear the music of the wheels,
I hear the wagoner's hoarse, harsh
voice urging the laboring steeds-
I see the horses pull and slip, urged
to more herculean deeds."
—Henry Lee Fisher

"I refer to him [Jost Herbach] and these incidents in this preface,
partly, I confess, from a modest pride of ancestry, but more
especially because in my judgement he was in all respects, a
model Pennsylvania-German gentleman of the olden times: a
faithful representative of the people whose quiet, simple, honest,
virtuous and industrious home life, I have made a humble, but I
fear, unsuccessful attempt, to delineate in the following pages."
—Henry Lee Fisher

Contents

Prologue

"To him, a farm was happiness, and paid for, it was bliss,
In Health and peace and honest toil
He turned and turned the rugged soil,
But well assured of this-
That rural life, though rough and hard,
Brings in this life, the best reward."

—Henry Lee Fisher

June 1828

Family farming is all about hard work, and it starts early in life. Farmers don't just grow crops—they grow workers. I must have been about four years of age when Ma took me to the end of a row of young cabbage plants. She pointed to the cabbage and said, "No pull-out!" Then she pointed to the weeds and said, "Pull out!" I worked at the task until it was completed. Another early responsibility was collecting eggs in the chicken house. At first, I was intimidated by Brewster the Rooster. He had a bloodred comb and wattles, fancy hackle feathers on his neck, tail feather swooped over his hind end. He was handsome, and he was big! As soon as I turned my back, he would spring at me with spurs, beak, and flapping wings. He left me with physical scars and a wounded pride. The problem was solved when I armed myself with a stout stick.

Out of the corner of my eye, I saw him launch his attack. As I turned, I swung that stick with all my strength and hit the sneaking fowl in midair, sending him tumbling to the ground. Surprised and disgruntled, he picked himself up, shook his body to restore his ruffled feathers, and perhaps his dignity, and scampered off. As long as

9

I had the stick, he would strut and prance in mock attack (for the benefit of his "harem"), but he stayed away from me.

Some might say that was a harsh childhood existence, but I was raised with the Pennsylvania Dutch work ethic, which stressed the value and satisfaction of hard work. As I grew older, my younger siblings assumed those tasks I had performed with the same sense of satisfaction as I had. I took pride in my new responsibilities of tending to livestock, plowing fields, and harvesting crops. As the Bible says, "That if any would not work, neither should he eat" (2 Thess. 3:10).

I am now eighty-seven years old and reminiscing the full, productive life I have been blessed with. My name is Jost Herbach. In my prime, I was six feet and two inches tall with reddish-blonde hair, blue eyes, and a ruddy complexion. I had a lean but well-muscled frame, and I was proud of my physical robustness. I am still grateful for the strength and good health I possess in my old age. By profession, I am a farmer—and proud of it—but this ordinary man has had some extraordinary experiences.

I had met and worked with the heroes of the age: George Washington and Ben Franklin. I hobnobbed with larger-than-life characters, like Daniel Boone and Daniel Morgan. I participated in a life-or-death struggle as a wagoner in the French and Indian War. As a captain, I saw action in the great revolutionary war to gain our freedom as a nation. I had the honor of having a leadership position in the Coetus of the Lutheran Church. My faith is very important to me. I also saw action in political wars as a legislator in the Pennsylvania State House of Representatives.

Of course, even the good life has its downsides. I have had my share of grief, suffering, and sorrow in my life. I have had the heart-wrenching task of burying two wives, all my siblings but one sister, and even two of my children. I have witnessed brutality, savagery, tyranny, and injustice, all of which will be apparent in the following pages. This is life—the good, the bad, and the ugly. It's how you cope and deal with these things that matters. That's what makes the man.

I am prompted to record these memories by one of my grandsons, Henry Lee Fisher, whose inquisitive mind is always seeking information about my life. A rarity among youth, he has esteem and respect for my age and experience. Henry has a natural affection, not only for me personally but also for the culture and traditions I represent. Often after a hearty helping of my favorite meal, *mosch-un-millich*, at his mother's table, we would retire to the parlor; and I would tell tales until his mother insisted he go to bed. His favorite subject was my participation in the Battle of the Monongahela in 1755.

This battle is the focus of the following pages. It includes events leading up to and following this historic event. It is my perspective as a young farmer-wagoner of Braddock's Defeat.

1

"Shining barrels of muskets, the excellent order of the
men, the cleanliness of their appearance, the joy depicted
on every face at being so near Fort Duquesne, the highest
object of their wishes—the music re-echoed through
the mountains. How brilliant the morning."
—Unknown eyewitness

"What am I doing here? Will I survive? Will any British survive?
Dear God help me! What should I do?"
—Jost Herbach

July 9, 1755

The day had started well enough. After weeks of struggling to cut a
road through a wilderness consisting of trees big enough for three
men to hide behind; of fallen timber tangles, rocks, and boulders;
of mucky swamps and steep grades that made our feet feel as heavy
as lead, we were finally within nine miles of our destination—Fort
Duquesne. We had not only struggled with the elements that weak-
ened our bodies but also the terror and fear of Indian atrocities that
afflicted our souls.

Frontiersmen regaled us with stories of horrific Indian actions
so vile, so cruel, they seemed inhuman. One such tale was the killing,
cooking, and eating of a British ally, Chief Meneskia of the Miami
tribe. They told in great detail of the setting of a giant kettle full of
water over a blazing fire. When it was fully boiling, they unceremo-
niously dumped the old chief in. They would argue among them-

selves as to whether he was dead or alive when they put him in and after about a half hour the savages began cutting off chunks to consume. That picture and others haunted our waking thoughts and our dreams at night.

But that was the past. We were still surrounded by wilderness, but today we forded the Monongahela River without any opposition. It was a widely held belief that this was the most likely time and place for a major French and Indian attack. There appeared to be no sign of the enemy, so perhaps the rumors were true. The French were few in number and afraid to leave the protection of their fort, and their Indian allies seeing the strength of our army had abandoned them.

The spirits of everyone from General Braddock down through the ranks to us wagoners shifted from despondency to cautious confidence. The contagion of fear was replaced with the smell of victory. This euphoria was heightened when General Braddock ordered the fifes and drums to play "The Grenadier March" as the men marched. The lively tune created a jocular and celebratory mood. The troops stepped a little lighter, and there was a growing atmosphere of self-assurance. *We can do this! We can capture Fort Duquesne!*

Our wagons were at the end of the column; and we were sharing in the high spirits among ourselves and even with Colonel Sir Peter Halkett and his men, whose assignment would be to protect us if attacked. John Finley, as usual, was recounting the wonders of "Kentuck-ee" to a very attentive Daniel Boone. A rather dower Daniel Morgan was cursing the British regulars under his breath while I said nothing. It all seemed so normal.

A single shot, barely audible over the music, changed the day and changed history. It was closely followed by a more discernible volley of gunfire. Colonel Halkett immediately assembled his men to form a line facing the gunfire. Everyone had an opinion on what was happening ahead of us.

Dan Boone was the first to expound. "By the sound of the volley, it is most likely the French are trying to slow our advance, but why they didn't do this as we crossed the river, I can't figure."

John Finley chimed in, "Naw, the Frogs is getting a taste of massed British firepower."

"Nope, the single shot was a rogue Indian trying to prove his bravery, and the volley was the skittish 44th regiment wasting powder and lead shooting at ghosts!" said Dan Morgan.

I just listened in awe because all these men had experience in fighting Indians; and I, being a fourteen-year-old farm boy (now wagoner) from York, Pennsylvania, had none. I hung on every word they said even when they disagreed with each other.

More shots rang out, and Indian war whoops could now be heard. They could not only be heard, but they were growing louder— closer! We each went to our own wagons to hobble and quiet our terrified horses.

Following the lead of my friends, I climbed into my wagon for cover and protection; but I could not help but peak over the side-board to see what was happening. At first, it was the sounds of battle rather than the sight of it; for the fighting was still far ahead, and smoke from musket fire enveloped the area in something akin to a heavy fog. Even the acrid smell of gunpowder came on us before we could see any of the fight.

The music had stopped, and the musket fire intensified. The cries of the wounded, dying, and terrified men increased, telling a story of growing confusion. I heard the pitiful cries of men calling for help, pleading for mercy, beseeching God, and calling for their mothers. The anguish of it squeezed my heart into a painful knot. Added to this was the unearthly squealing sound of wounded and dying horses along with officers barking orders to their men. Above all of this, the Indian war cries pierced through the other noises and sounded like banshees being released from hell. The sounds told us what we couldn't see—the army was in chaos.

As the battle came closer to our position, I could make out the red coats of the British troops. I could see advancing troops colliding with retreating soldiers. I could see lines of defense disintegrating and men forming into small circles or running for their lives. I also began to see the hostiles moving from tree to tree to outflank us, shooting from behind cover as they advanced. It was becoming a "running" battle.

Then out of the mist, running toward me was the young drummer Tim Murphy. Back at Fort Cumberland, he and I had bonded because he was a youngster too (he was twelve). He had flaming-red hair, twinkling mischievous eyes, a somewhat prominent nose (like mine), and a winning smile. I liked him. He was the little drummer boy. But now the expression on his face was fear. His drum bounced off his churning legs as he ran. His drumsticks were beating the air in his flailing arms. His mouth was formed in a scream I could not distinguish in the din of battle. I wanted to run to him, to save him.

Out of the smoke right behind him came a savage with half his face painted red and the other half black, a tomahawk in his hand and a vicious war cry from his distorted mouth—a vision from hell! He overtook Tim and drove his weapon into his back. Tim's eyes opened in a wide expression of disbelief. Before he hit the ground, the Indian had dropped the tomahawk and produced a knife that encircled Tim's head, from his forehead around above the ears to the nape of his neck. In one swift movement, he grabbed the hair and ripped off Tim's scalp. In a bloodlust, the savage held it high with blood dripping down his arm and a triumphant scream on his lips. My stomach churned, and I wanted to throw up; but I would see more of this and much worse on this accursed day.

I saw a badly wounded officer whose hands extended toward the sky—whether to plead to God or to obstruct the blow he knew was coming from the blood-covered Indian standing over him, I do not know. The savage plunged his knife into the man's chest and removed his heart. He took the still-beating organ, bit into it, and chewed it as blood coated his chin and arms. This time, I did vomit.

Scenes like these were repeated many times. Too many times. My mind and heart experienced many emotions that were strong and conflicting. I felt fear, fright, repulsion, and disgust, but also anger and bitterness. I felt sick but also sad. One sight brought true tears of grief and sadness. Colonel Sir Peter Halkett was doing his best to rally his troops. He was the most likeable of the British officers. He treated us fairly. He was authoritative but not condescending to us. For these same reasons, he was popular among his troops.

I saw him collapse from a musket wound. His youngest son, Lieutenant James Halkett, ran to his father's aid. As he sat cradling his father's head in his arms, he himself was shot and collapsed dead on top of his father. This touched me in a way different from the other atrocities happening around me. The affection of father and son and their deaths seemed so tragic. Daniel Boone also saw this tragedy play out before us, and when one of the heathens attempted to scalp the duo, he obliterated his head with a shot from his firearm he called Old Tick Licker because he said he could shoot a tick off the nose of a bear.

Seeing Daniel make that shot, snapped me out of my indolence. I had been immobilized by the carnage taking place around me. *The musket! I have a musket!* I checked to see if it was primed and loaded. I peeked over the sideboard of the wagon. There were targets, Indians, everywhere. I picked out a savage running from one tree to the cover of another. I aimed and squeezed the trigger. It looked like he fell from a wound, but he could have been leaping to safety. To this day, I am not sure which it was.

I reloaded and again looked over the sideboard. I was greeted by the sound of a thud hitting the board just next to my face. I had made myself a target by firing my weapon. I felt pain in my forehead and a warm liquid running down my face. *Had I been hit?* I reached for my face and wood splinters just above my left eye. The liquid was blood coming from the superficial wound. I pulled out the bigger splinters. The battle had definitely reached me. I hunkered down for a few minutes and then peeked over the sideboard again.

My reeling mind could hardly comprehend what I saw next. It was Colonel Washington, still on a mount, extolling maybe one hundred men in a somewhat organized retreat. One line of men would fire their weapons and then fall back to reload as the second line would then do the same. This was repeated over and over. The line was ragged, and they took some losses; but their semblance of order made it possible to bring with them some wounded, including General Braddock himself as well as other wounded officers. Shots whizzed all around Colonel Washington as he rode from one group of soldiers to another, ordering, coaxing, and encouraging them.

What was so amazing was that just two days ago, he was lying in the bed of my wagon, emaciated and feverish with dysentery. He was pale, thin, and still feverish. He was so wiped out from the overuse of his bowels, he put a pillow on his saddle to ease the pain. In the midst of all the hell going on around me, another emotion enveloped me: admiration. Admiration for a young man—a warrior—driven by duty and honor (and maybe ambition) to be a leader.

More shots hit my wagon, and I saw a bullet shatter the arm of a fellow wagoner named Lewin. Suddenly Daniel Boone was next to my wagon mounted on a horse. "Jost, cut your harness, mount your horse, and save yourself. Ride out of here." As quick as he appeared, he was gone.

My muddled mind was racing. *What am I doing here? Will I survive? Will any British survive? Dear God help me. What should I do?*

2

"The family home is a divine institution; a heaven-
like retreat in our earthly pilgrimage; the scene of births
and deaths, of hopes and fears, joys and sorrows."
—Henry Lee Fisher

"And God blessed them, and God said unto them, be fruitful
and multiply and replenish the earth, and subdue it: and
have dominion over the fish of the sea, and over the fowl of
the air, and every living that that moves upon the earth."
—Genesis 1:28 (KJV)

May 1755

Plowing is hard work. Controlling a team of powerful horses as they
pull a plow through dirt, rocks, and roots, requires strength. As does
removing those same rocks and roots from the field. Walking on
clods of freshly turned earth necessitates constant attention and nim-
bleness of foot.

I was big for my age and quite capable of handling a plow and
its team of horses. It was exceptionally warm for a spring day, and
sweat covered my body and was stinging my eyes. I wiped the perspiration from my forehead with the sleeve of my shirt and decided
it was time for a break. I was thinking of the horses as well as myself;
they were also working hard. There was a cool, clear limestone spring
near the field. It was like a little oasis. The water tasted sweet and
cooled my damp skin.

As I rested, I took the opportunity to enjoy the wonders of
God's creation all around me. Tauser, the family dog, was a giant

bundle of hair and slobber that had accompanied me to the field. He had long since lost interest in his surroundings and returned to the farm. Before he left, he had busted out a covey of bobwhite quail. As I sat, I heard these meaty little game birds calling their cheery bob-white whistle to regather their family group. I imitated their whistle tune and enjoyed when they answered me.

Other birds soon caught my attention as they added their voices to nature's musical symphony. Robins were happily tweeting in between gorging their beaks with earthworms from the freshly turned soil. The bossy wrens seemed to be scolding everybody. Woodpeckers were like drummers keeping the beat with their tapping of trees while looking for an insect snack. Even the raucous sounds of crows and blue jays couldn't ruin the musical entertainment.

Birds were also part of the colorful scenery. Those same noisy blue jays always came in groups like hordes of wild Indians with their war whoops, intimidating and spreading chaos in the bird world. Their bright blue color made up for what they lacked in personality. The brightness of the bluebirds was even more radiant than that of the jays; and they had a much better, friendlier disposition. The red hue of the cardinal outshone them all. In contrast, even the chick-adees and sparrows added their own subtle colors and calls to the scene.

Nature's masterpiece included the colors and aromas of the trees, shrubs, and wildflowers around me. The blooming fruit trees in the nearby orchard added color and rich smells to the environ-ment. The woodland phlox, with their pink and purple flowers, and honeysuckle bushes, with white and orange flowers, conveyed a scent almost like a sickeningly sweet perfume. All the senses seemed to be assaulted by nature, and it was wonderful.

Last, but not least, was the soil. I loved the earthy smell of freshly tilled ground. I loved to feel it, hold it in my hand, and squeeze it through my fingers. I never tired of this. As I resumed my plowing, all my senses absorbed the beauty and life surrounding me. When I finished plowing, I looked with a feeling of accomplishment at the result—a field ready to be seeded with corn. I congratulated myself with a hearty "Job well done!" Working and living in the Kreutz Creek Valley of York County, Pennsylvania, was indeed rewarding.

Suddenly the peace and tranquility was shattered by the barking of Tauser, who almost knocked me over in his exuberance. My younger brother, Henry (age eleven), was trying to shout through his labored breathing, "MA...SAYS...DINNER WILL BE...READY...IN... HALF AN...HOUR!" After a pause, he continued, "GEORGE AND LUDWIG [our two oldest brothers]...ARE VISITING...AND...THERE IS BIG NEWS...FROM PHILADELPHIA!" He was breathless from his hard run to fetch me. He stood panting, hands on his knees. I gave his head an affectionate rub. Henry idolized me, and I had a special brotherly bond with him. Some folks called him Little Jost because he looked like a younger version of myself.

"Catch your breath while I unhitch the horses, and you can ride one of them back to the stable."

His bright smile radiated. "I'd love that."

It is a funny thing about brothers—we would all defend each other to the death but often related to each other as enemies. My oldest brothers, George (age twenty-nine) and Ludwig (age twenty-eight), were almost like strangers to me. They had moved to the western part of York County to establish their own homesteads when I was still small. They purchased their land from the locally famous Christian Lau, who was the first white settler in that area. In fact, he originally lived in a wigwam among the Indians. His children's early playmates were redskins.

It is said he paid the natives a fair price for the land, which also bought him peace with the tribes. He prospered and built a mill on Codorus Creek. The fertile bottom land and the availability of a mill are what attracted my brothers to the area. Their visits were rare, so this was indeed a special occasion.

While on the topic of brothers, Jacob (age twenty-five) was still living at home with us. I cared for him, but to me, he was my nemesis—a thorn, an agitation, and a challenge. It seemed he was always picking on me and bossing me around. He was the bane of my existence. We were as different as two brothers could be. Although much younger, I was taller than him (and better looking), but I lacked his muscular bulk. He was short and stocky with dark hair and heavy eyebrows that made him appear even older than his twenty-five years. He had recently, and finally, found a sweetheart; and I hoped he would soon marry and *leave* to develop his own homestead.

We competed in everything. We wrestled and fought, sometimes in friendly banter but often in a serious manner. I remember once, after a long day of plowing, I returned to the barn to groom and care for the horses. As I completed the work, I was covered in sweat, but the horses had clean and shiny coats. I stood back and thought, *Good work. Done at last!*

Suddenly, a shower of straw cascaded over me and the horses, and there stood Jacob with a pitchfork in his hand and a huge smirk on his face. He said, "Better clean up them horses. Supper will be ready soon!"

I lunged at him, yelling, "*Klootzak* [asshole]!" (In anger I often reverted to Pennsylvania Dutch.)

I caught him around the legs, and he fell backward into a fresh pile of horse dung. I was on top of him in a flash, trying to shove his face into another pile of steaming manure. As he struggled to get up, his elbow cracked my nose, which sent my blood splattering all over us. Shit and blood in a fight equals "no quarter," but before any more damage could be done, Pa separated us.

Pa's anger was a fearsome thing to behold. He gritted his teeth, and his eyes bulged out of his red face. He also spoke Pennsylvania Dutch when he was angered, and *klootzak* was just one of many unkind names hurled at us. Strange thing is it wasn't the scolding or whippings or the increased work load that hurt the most. It was the feeling we had let him down. We knew he loved us and wanted us to grow up to be men of good character. I realize now these mock battles were preparing me for more serious challenges that would come my way in the future.

As Henry and I approached the farm, we were greeted with snorts, grunts, whinnies, and moos from the barnyard and the smell of wood smoke from the chimney. Our home consisted of a large room with a huge stone hearth, candles on the mantel, and the family musket hanging above it. (We kept another musket over the front entrance just for quick retrieval, if needed.) Mother's pride and joy was a rocking chair given to her by her family, and it was one that calmed many a baby and small child with its soothing rocking motion. Father had a large comfortable wooden chair with a foot stool. A small table was next to it with his Bible, clay pipe, and favorite mug.

A large plain table and benches that could easily accommodate ten people were in the center of the room. Several chests containing linens, blankets, and clothes abutted the walls and also served as additional seating. A crude cabinet stood against the wall adjacent to the fireplace. It contained all the utensils Ma needed to prepare her wonderful hearty meals. Peg hooks adorned either side of the entrance door to accommodate clothing and hats. Boots were generally left outside on the porch. A smaller attached room was our parents' bedroom, and we were never allowed to go in there. A large loft was our sleeping quarters.

The house was always neat and tidy. The atmosphere was simple yet comfortable and inviting. Barns and outbuildings were in some ways more important to farmers than even their own homes and often got more attention. Harvesting, preserving, and storing food for family and livestock often got first consideration and attention because they impacted quality of life and even survival. Our house was our home, and we felt secure in it.

As we entered the house, my stomach growled, and my mouth watered as the pungent aroma of sauerkraut (fermented cabbage) filled my nostrils. Pa jokingly called sauerkraut the food of the Teutonic gods. I just called it plain good! In addition, there was a pork roast, pickled hard boiled eggs, and potatoes. There was also bread, butter, and apple butter in abundance. For dessert, Ma made an apple crisp pie that was to die for. Spring water and milk cooled in the springhouse was used to wash down the nourishment. Ma went all out for the company, and we all benefited.

Pa prayed over the meal, as he always did; and we all ate like we hadn't seen any food for a week. After the meal, the table was cleared, and Pa and the older brothers lit their pipes and filled the room with a hazy cloud and the smell of tobacco. Then we finally got down to the big news. Ben Franklin was coming to Kreutz Creek!

3

"Whereas, one hundred and fifty waggons, with four horses to each waggon, and fifteen hundred saddle or pack horses are wanted for the services of his majesty's forces now about to rendezvous at Will's Creek, and his excellency General Braddock having been pleased to contract me for the hire of the same, I hereby give notice that I shall attend for that purpose at Lancaster from this day to next Wednesday evening, and at York from next Thursday morning till Friday evening, where I shall be ready to agree for wagons and teams, or single horses on the following terms, viz: 1. That there shall be paid for each waggon, with four good horses and a driver, fifteen shillings per diem and for each able horse with a packsaddle…two shillings per diem… 2. That the pay commences from the time of their joining the forces at Will's Creek… 3. Each waggon and team, and…every horse, is to be valued by indifferent persons chosen between me and the owner, and in case of loss of any waggon, team, or other horse in the service, the price according to such valuations is to be allowed and paid. 4. Seven days pay in advance…remainder to be paid by General Braddock… 5. No No drivers of waggons…are on any account to be called upon to do the duty of soldiers, or be otherwise employed than in conducting or taking care of their carriages or horses."

—Benjamin Franklin's advertisement

April 1755

The good news was Benjamin Franklin came to our little valley. The bad news was he brought General Sir John Saint Clair with him. Mr. Franklin was perhaps the most famous man in the colonies. He was well known in the German community partially because in 1732, he published the first German newspaper, *Die Philadelphische Zeiting*. This contributed to competitors starting their own German publications, which greatly benefited our community.

Our family spoke and read both German and English, so we enjoyed Mr. Franklin's other publications as well. (Pa held to the practical view—since we were living in English lands, we should be able to communicate in English.) *Poor Richard's Almanac* and the *Pennsylvania Gazette* were enjoyed by our family; and they were used by Ma as teaching tools, along with the Bible. Both of these contained not only news and helpful information but also wit, satire, and entertainment.

In May of 1754, he captured the attention and interests of the colonists when he published an essay for the unification of the colonies to combat growing Indian and French threats. Though rejected at the time, the idea would take root in the American Revolution, as did his illustration of a snake cut into pieces with each piece being labeled one of the colonies. Underneath was the slogan "Join or Die." He was currently Postmaster General of the colonies and was recognized for the efficiency of mail delivery.

In 1755, Immanuel Kant, no intellectual slacker himself, called Franklin the "Prometheus of our time." He was a writer, printer, politician, philosopher, scientist, postmaster, inventor, humorist and statesman. Impressive as this list was, as a young boy, I was most attracted to his personality. Not particularly impressive to look at, he possessed a charm, a sense of self-awareness, almost an aura about him. He had a friendly demeanor and made you feel as if he cared about you. He had the presence of mind to remember the names of people he met. Although I said very little to him, I was most flattered when he addressed me by name on subsequent encounters. He was indeed most agreeable...and crafty, as we would soon discover.

His companion, General Sir John Saint Clair was the Quarter Master General in charge of procuring supplies for General Braddock's army. He had a handsome but cruel face and the paunchy body of an older man. His demeanor was condescending and rude. To me there was nothing likeable or commendable about him. Although he was a Scotsman, he had served in the Prussian light cavalry called the Hussars. In Europe, Hussars were feared by the people for their looting and pillaging. They were as intimidating then as he was now (he was wearing his Hussar uniform). It soon became apparent that Franklin was the "carrot" and Saint Clair was the "stick" in their bid to influence the local population.

The meeting was held at our local Lutheran church since it was a convenient location. Franklin began.

"Friends and neighbors, I am here as a representative of His Majesty the King, Governor Morris, and General Braddock. As you have read in my post, the army needs wagons, teams, drivers, and horses to defend us against the Indian and French threat. This is a grand opportunity for you as individuals to make some coin, almost risk free, and as a community to prove your loyalty to the Crown, which some people doubt. Are there any questions about the provisions outlined in my posted bill?"

There were disgruntled murmurings from the crowd. Pa, never being shy about matters of pride and possessions, was the first to speak.

"We lead our life quietly in our own way, but we are loyal citizens of the Crown and the Commonwealth of Pennsylvania. But we do have some concerns about your proposal. In item number three, concerning payment upon loss of possessions, who will be guaranteeing the reimbursement?"

There were mumbles of agreement to the question from the crowd.

Franklin affably responded, "That's a good question, and I am glad you asked it. The Commonwealth of Pennsylvania will be backing the reimbursement."

The volume of discontent among the gathering increased substantially.

Pa responded, "Those pacifist Quakers in Philadelphia are not to be trusted. They are very tight with spending on anything, but they are particularly opposed to spending on war. You'll have to do better than that for us to part with the horses and wagons so valuable to our livelihood."

Loud assents from the audience followed Pa's statement. Mr. Franklin motioned for the crowd to get quiet. When the noise subsided, he said, "I will use my own personal fortune to back any payments for loss."

The people were astounded at this, and one man spoke up, "You mean, you have enough confidence in this expedition's success to risk your own money?"

"I do," he quickly replied. This calmed the crowd and seemed to settle that issue.

Unusual at the time for a woman to speak out in public, but not unusual for Ma, she was the next to speak. She spoke on behalf of all the women there. She wasn't worried so much about possessions, but she was worried about kin—about people.

"One of my sons will be a driver, and I am concerned for his well-being. Does your personal guarantee extend to the provisions in point number five that wagoners will not be called upon to fight or do any labor other than caring for their wagons and horses?"

There were more murmurs of assent, particularly from the mothers in the crowd.

General Saint Clair began to step forward, but before he could get a word out of his open mouth, Franklin put his arm out to restrain him. As he did this, he said, "Madam, the horses and wagons will be at the rear of the columns of soldiers, away from danger. They will be as safe as riding the road to Lancaster."

Ma became silent but did press him some more about it at our farm, where the two visitors had supper with us.

The crowd still seemed unsettled and hesitant to make any commitments. This is when the crafty Mr. Franklin, all smiles, alluded to his companion.

"General Saint Clair has advised me that General Braddock, and indeed the British Crown, questions your loyalty. I assured him you are grateful for the opportunities afforded you here in Pennsylvania. That you are honorable men who would willingly support the defense of the colony against the heathens. I hope I am not wrong in this sentiment!"

Then Saint Clair did step forward, terrifying in his Hussar uniform and hat. The hardness etched on his face showed no hint of kindness or mercy.

"General Braddock has a mind to commandeer what he needs, and I will be the man to enforce those orders if given." This was the "stick".

His very presence in that uniform was a real reminder of the damage he could do.

Franklin stepped forward again (the return of the "carrot") and in a calming voice said, "Now, now, there will be no need for that. These fine people will see the many benefits of money in hand and protection from the savages."

The assembly grudgingly seemed to approve, and individuals began to sign on to the program.

4

"Each man is really three men: the man he thinks he is;
the man others think he is and the man he really is."
                                    —Jean de La Fontaine (poet)

May 1755

That evening, the dinner went well. Mr. Franklin's congeniality cap-tivated us all. He expounded on many topics, including our favorites, agriculture and husbandry. To his credit, he did not dominate the conversation but asked insightful questions about our life. Even the children were given attention as he spoke with us in a kindly manner. He referred to me as young Jost. Amazed I was only fourteen, he said I could easily pass for seventeen or even eighteen. I puffed up with pride.

He asked, "What are your goals and aspirations in this life?"

"I want to marry Sarah Kauffman and have a farm and family of my own, like Pa."

He smiled. "Very noble goals I am sure you will attain. But remember, opportunities abound here for anyone willing to dream big and work hard."

I was somewhat taken aback by his remark, which seemed to suggest I might accomplish more.

When he asked Henry what he wanted to be when he grew up, he responded, "I want to be like Jost."

Franklin patted his arm. "That is indeed a worthy goal and the greatest compliment you can give your brother."

For all of Mr. Franklin's efforts to put us at ease, Saint Clair seemed intent at putting us on edge. He sat quietly, the sharp features of his face making him look like a hawk ready to pounce on a rabbit. His demeanor softened somewhat while eating Ma's meal. The main course was chicken and dumplings with the usual side dishes and dessert. He actually smiled a little, at least as much as his dour lips would allow, as he ate. Ma (the rabbit) had conquered Saint Clair (the hawk).

Mr. Franklin also ate heartily, filling his extended middle-aged paunch to full capacity. It had been a full and exciting day, but tomorrow would bring its own excitement and new challenges.

The next day, at breakfast, Pa made a shocking announcement. "Jost will be taking the team and wagon to Will's Creek."

The whole family was stunned. Jacob was so enraged he could hardly speak. His face was red and through flying spittle, he finally blurted out, "I am the oldest and most fit here." He looked at me with loathing. "He is just a boy!" He emphasized *boy* like it was a dirty word.

Henry shouted, "I DON'T WANT JOST TO GO!"

Ma reached out her hand to console him. Her face was saddened and conflicted. I never saw her at a loss for words, but she couldn't favor one son over another. Still, I knew she didn't want me to go. She loved and respected Pa enough to accept his decision.

Jacob continued his almost unintelligible rant when suddenly Pa slammed his fist on the table with such force the trenchers and mugs jumped and rattled. Not only the table but the whole floor shook. Pa had our undivided attention.

"I will—I have decided what is best for the family. Our workforce will be cut almost in half during spring planting and although Jost is a good worker, I will need a stronger, more experienced man to pick up the slack."

My heart sank at these words.

"Jacob, you are to be married soon, and I'll not do anything to jeopardize your wedding. There will be no separation time from Dorcas. This is final. Jost can do it. Jost will go!"

I puffed up with pride and said, "I can do it, Pa. I won't let you down."

Actually, for me it was a moment of truth. It was a time to face the conflicts and even contradictions I held secretly deep inside. Jacob was always tearing me down, making me feel inadequate, like I could do nothing right. On the other hand, Henry held me in such high esteem I was fearful of letting him down. Because of my height, all my life people, except Jacob, expected much of me. Sometimes, it was more than I thought I could deliver. I felt like a boy in a man's body. The responsibilities placed on me often weighed heavy on me.

Responsibility. Hearing that word brought me out of my thoughts and back to reality.

Pa was saying, "It will be work and responsibility." There was that word.

Henry ran to me as I arose from my seat and hugged me around the waist with his head in my chest. "I want to go with you. I can help."

I returned his hug warmly. "I will miss you like crazy, but I won't be gone long. And you are needed here."

"That's right," said Pa. "You'll have your regular chores and much more with Jost gone. You will have your own responsibilities." (Ouch. There is that word again.)

So it was settled. I would be going further from home, for a longer period of time than any of my siblings had ever done. *Alone.*

5

"Three or four such farmers as cannot separately spare
from business of their Plantations a wagon and four horses
and driver may do it together, one furnishing the wagon,
another one or two horses and another the driver."

—Ben Franklin

Of all the animals on the farm, I found the horses to be the most fascinating. It was as if God designed them specifically for man's use. With their strength, they could pull heavy objects and equipment; and with their speed, they could transport a person faster than any man could run. They have personalities, like people. They can be bold, shy, lazy, docile, aggressive, mean, affectionate, stubborn, and distrustful. I became attached to them in a fashion similar to my fondness for the family dog, Tauser. Just as their personalities differ, so do their physical appearance. Big, small, short, or tall—each had distinctive features making them individuals.

Always practical, Pa used these characteristics to name our horses. We had six horses on our farm (or plantation, as Mr. Franklin called it). They were bred for strength and endurance rather than speed. They had bulging muscles in their chest and shoulders and also in their rumps. Their names were simple and efficient: Black, Brown, Blaze, Socks, Spots, and Camel. Each animal recognized its own name, and so did we.

When Pa said to use Black and Spots to plow a field, we knew he meant the black horse and the spotted horse. You may ask, "Why the name Camel?" Camel was a plain, ordinary-looking horse that had a distinct hump on his back, making him painful to ride bareback. But he was a strong, dependable workhorse.

Two of our horses were old and used sparingly. With it being the spring (plowing and planting season), we could only afford to provide two horses and our wagon for British use. Since my brothers George and Ludwig were just starting out on their own farms, they had fewer resources, but each contributed a horse to our team. This provided a challenge to me.

I was to take Black, a gelding, and the mare Brown to be the anchors for my team. They were both strong, healthy, gentle horses and a pleasure to work with. But I was adding two unknowns to the team. They were George's Dusty and Ludwig's Saddle, a mostly white mare with a large patch of brown hair covering it's back shaped like a saddle.

Mixing strange animals together can present a problem. There is often a struggle to determine who is at the top of the pecking order. Geldings sometimes "think" they are still stallions (poor guys) and want to assert themselves. Mares…well…mares are females and can be very bossy. At first, Dusty and Saddle were somewhat nervous and jittery; and we got off to a bad start (or you might say on the wrong foot) when Dusty, while prancing around, stepped on my foot. Believe me. It was painful.

My job was to help them adjust to their new situation and get them to work together as a team. To do this, I bribed them with carrots and other treats (This is where the "carrot" approach to solving problems originated from!) If they didn't respond to this as I wanted, I would use a stern, not harsh, voice with a tug on their halter to get their attention. The combination of feeding, talking quietly, and grooming eventually won their trust. They love grooming. It must have felt better to them than scratching an itch.

I also checked their teeth and hooves. Horses that can't eat or are lame are worse than useless to the task at hand. I continued to do all these things while on our journey. As the bond and trust between myself and my charges developed, as they were responding positively toward working with each other and being a team, I then turned my attention to the wagon.

6

"These were the thrifty farmers teams,
That wagoned only now and then;
They made their trips in winter-time;
They trudged along through rime and grime
And hurried through it, back again;
An annual trip or two they made,
And drove a sort of coastwise trade."

—Henry Lee Fisher

Our wagon had seen its share of wear and tear. Over the years, it was often pulled into fields to harvest crops and into woods to bring in logs and firewood. Occasionally, trips were made to the Yorktown or Lancaster markets to sell or buy goods. We even took trips to Baltimore harbor once in a while because we got better prices there. Despite its heavy use, the wagon was well maintained.

All the farm wagons in the valley are made in Lancaster. They are called Conestoga wagons and are exceptionally well engineered and quality built. The wagons are designed with various types of wood: tough oak for the perch, springy hickory for the spokes, non-splitting sour gum for the hubs, and half-inch pine or poplar boards for the body.

Its shape reminds me of the Egyptian skiffs or boats that plied the ancient Nile River. I remember Bible study illustrations of these vessels that looked like a big smile when viewed from the side. Our wagon looked like that vessel, with the bow or tips cut off. The bed is about twelve feet long on the bottom and fourteen feet long on the top. The graceful boat shape of the body, deeply curved with the raking ends so the load would settle to the middle, made it perfect for going up and down hills. The depth of the bed is three feet; and the width is four feet, allowing space for about a ton of transports.

The front wheels are forty-two inches in diameter, and the rear wheels are fifty-two inches. The wheel is composed of a hub connected by spokes to the ring or wheel. They are all held together by a "tire," which is a two-inch strip of heated iron wrapped around the circumference. When cooled rapidly, it shrank to hold everything together tightly. This process is called sweating. It is common practice to "kick the tire" to make sure it is secure. If it is loose, then repairs or a new wheel is needed. Our wagon wheels were all studded with small metal "nubs" that added traction and helped navigate rough fields and terrain. Wheels are removed and greased every 100 miles.

The tong is connected to the wagon with a heavy pin shaped as a hammer and often doubled as a tool. Only local farm wagons had this unique practical feature. The leather harness was draped over and attached to the horses. The harness was attached to the tong. There is no seat on our wagon. Space and weight were too valuable to be taken by the driver, so the driver—me—walked. I walk on the left side of the wagon with reins in hand attached to each horse's halter and bit. By the dexterous maneuvering of my fingers, each horse is individually controlled. It takes practice to be a good driver.

The body of our wagon is held together by wrought iron hasps that are both practical and decorative in nature. Our wagon, like all others in the area, is painted a light but bright blue called peacock blue. All the running gear, including tong and wheels, are vermilion red. The ironwork is black. This is all topped off with a white homespun cover stretched over eight hoops to protect the cargo. Altogether it makes a pleasing appearance, considering it is farm equipment. Pa always takes great pains to keep it in tip-top shape and looking nice. "I don't want people to think we are remiss in the care of what God has so graciously provided us."

7

"Each wagon and team, and every horse, is to be valued by indifferent persons chosen between me and the owner, and in case of loss of any wagon team, or other horse in the service, the price according to such valuations is to be allowed and paid."
—Ben Franklin

"Well done!" Those words from my father were music to my ears. Pa had inspected the team and wagon thoroughly. He checked the axles, every hinge and every fitting, the harness, and the horses; and of course, he "kicked the tires." I had worked hard to prepare for my journey, and Pa was satisfied that everything was in good order. The next step before leaving was to get an appraisal for valuation, in case of damage or loss.

If you recall, the evaluation was to be made by parties chosen by Mr. Franklin and the owners. When we arrived at the appointed appraisal site, there was a lot of commotion. Urbanus Aschenbrenner was leading the mob. He was known for his aggressive nature and coarse manner of speaking. His face was red and hard looking, like it was made of leather and topped with an unkempt patch of gray hair. His arms were massive, and his hands were as rough as rawhide. His stout body rested on a pair of bow-legged stumps.

His many years of farming showed in every feature of his body. He was a typical German farmer, except he did not attend church. In his rage, he sometimes shifted back and forth between Pennsylvania Dutch and English, but he was very definitely making his meaning known.

"That amount ain't even half the value of this here outfit. I couldn't replace even one of my horses for the meager sum you say my whole team is worth. It's thievery! I'll drive the lot into hell myself before I'll ever deal with you two crooks!"

He turned to the crowd and continued, "How can we get a fair deal when we have these"—he pointed his thumb over his back at the targets of his remarks—"two so-called indifferent persons making the valuations."

He was referring to William Franklin, Benjamin's son, and John Read, Benjamin's brother-in-law.

"No one ask me if these fellas was acceptable to me. Talk about keepin' it in the family. Hell, they for sure ain't lookin' out for my interests or yours! They are keepin' valuations low to protect their family wealth. Damn! I will not tolerate it. No, sir, I will not be a party to this thievery!"

Voices came out of the crowd making threats like "Let's send them off with a boot up their behinds!" and "Anybody got any tar and feathers?"

Both men, Read and Franklin, were red faced and had perspiration falling of their faces even though it was a cool spring day. They were definitely nervous and maybe even fearful, but they stood their ground.

William addressed the crowd. "Quiet please! Let me address your concerns. Remember these valuations only matter if loss occurs, which is highly unlikely. Wagons and teams will not be anywhere near the fighting. Also, you are being paid a fair per diem fee for the use of your teams. Finally, remember if not for my father, General Sir John Saint Clair would be here right now confiscating your property for little or no recompense for you."

The crowd quieted. Each farmer bargained to get his best deal. They were not happy, but the valuations were a little higher than before the altercation. An uneasy truce settled in, and the task was completed.

When our turn came, William looked up from his paperwork and asked, "Are you the Johannes Herbach that entertained my father for supper when he was here?"

Pa responded he was and how much he enjoyed the evening with his father.

Looking at me, he said, "And you must be young Jost?"

I was flabbergasted and happily responded, "Yes."

William continued, "Father likes people who are industrious and achievers and was very impressed with both of you. He also spoke very highly of Mrs. Herbach's cooking. He said it was a delicious and hearty meal. The best of his trip to York and Lancaster."

We couldn't help but notice we received a higher valuation for our team and wagon than most others did. I guess it does pay to know people in high places!

8

"Each of us is born into a world that we did not make, and it
is only with the greatest effort, and often at a very great cost,
that we are ever able to change that world for the better."
—Wilford M. McClay (historian)

I was on my way. I was hauling corn to feed my team and for the
livestock at Wills Creek. I also had a substantial food stash for myself.
Once I reached Wills Creek, I was to be fed by the army; but until
then, I had johnny cakes, dried apples, fresh apples, carrots, potatoes,
and turnips from the ground cellar and hard-boiled eggs and dried
meat. I also had a tool kit, a jack, spare horseshoes, and nails.

The trip from York to Carlisle was somewhat lonely and uneventful. The road was safe and in good condition. I traveled with Urbanus
Aschenbrenner, Matt Laird, and Michael and Jacob Hoover. They
were all older than me, and though cordial, they mostly excluded
me from their inner circle. Unfortunately, Urbanus took me under
his wing. I say unfortunately because he was the unhappiest, most
negative person to be around.

Nothing suited. If you gave him an apple, it was too small or to
shriveled or tasteless. There was never a thank-you. It seemed every
other word out of his mouth was cursing or swearing. He was a miserable person and an even more miserable traveling companion. It
wasn't as if I had someone to talk to, but rather I was someone to be
talked at. I really did feel alone and scared, but my pride wouldn't let
it show.

When we reached Carlisle, I was shocked when each wagoner,
including myself, was issued a musket. It was a contract musket that
was forty-two inches long and fired a .69 caliber shot. We were also

given a powder horn. I knew how to use the firearm, for I did a lot of hunting in the hills surrounding the farm; but I couldn't figure why we were given a weapon. We had been assured we would see no combat. I suddenly became aware of the potential precarious situation I had been placed in.

There was a discussion as to which was the best route to take to Wills Creek. Some favored going south to Frederick and then west while others liked going west on the new Burd Road to Raystown and then south along Wills Mountain to Wills Creek. Urbanus chose the Frederick route, so I chose the Burd Road to get away from him. You could say he took the low road, and I took the high road. Little did I know, this choice would lead to a new nemesis that made Urbanus look like a saint. I was being a man, making my own decisions, on my own behalf, and would have to live with the consequences.

Burd Road was actually under construction at the time and was named after the overseer James Burd. The road was ninety miles long and paralleled Kittatinny Mountain before ascending it to a broad flat plain that ended at the foot of Tuscarora Mountain. One of our biggest hurdles was the climb up Sidling Hill. We eventually passed through the Tussey Mountain to parallel the Juniata River to Raystown. From there, we turned south along Wills Mountain to arrive at Wills Creek or Fort Cumberland as it was now being called.

Things were sour from the very beginning. We were each assigned a place in line. I was located behind one of the earliest professional teamsters, who were called Regulars (or Reg'lars as they pronounced it). His name was Tine Elliot, and he had it out for me before we even formally spoke to one another. His wagon looked exactly like mine—even the colors were the same. The difference was his wagon was much larger than mine. It was longer, deeper, wider and had a team of six matched horses. He was not a farmer but made his living hauling freight from Boston to New York, to Philadelphia, to Baltimore, and beyond.

I began to question myself. Was there something wrong with me? Why was I a target of the unlovely—the evil? My brother Jacob now looked like a "prince among men" next to Urbanus, who now looked almost a refined gentleman compared to Tine Elliot.

Tine Elliot…Where do I begin? Tine was short with sticks for legs. At the time, men's stockings were tight so they could show off their muscular calves to the ladies. Tine had none—calves, that is. You would think he would have muscular legs from all the walking he did. Instead, his stick legs supported a torso that gave the appearance of his being eight months with child (or maybe with twins). I suppose this was due to his heavy drinking. His arms had some muscle, which was probably from working the harness reins.

The further up his body you went, the worse it got. His face had big chubby pink cheeks. His eyes were small and beady; and one eye would occasionally wander off on its own, like it had a mind of its own. His head was mostly bald with a few tufts of wispy gray hair. His ears had large lobes, out of proportion with his other features. Finally, he had thin lips, which constantly held a cigar in them. In some ways, he looked like he was made with leftover parts. By the way, he called his cigar a stogie, a name that caught on generally because he drove a "Conastogie" wagon! Out of his mouth came a squeaky yet raspy sound that was irritating no matter what he was saying.

I was minding my own business when an irritating sound called out. "Hey, Pretty boy!" I wasn't even sure it was directed to me until he said, "Hey, you, pretty boy with the pretty golden locks!"

Up to that point, I had never spoken to the man, yet he was calling me out.

"Where'd you git that baby wagon and them ugly hosses, or is they mules?"

I didn't know how to respond. I was incredulous. As I compared our two rigs, there was no question his was larger with a handsome set of six matched horses. Next to his "Pa" wagon, my rig looked a "Ma" wagon or even a "baby" wagon, but this was true of the majority of farm wagons there. I muttered to myself and kicked the dirt with my boot.

Finally, I replied, "We have no call for an oversized wagon on our farm, and these four horses have more than enough individual strength—and beauty—to get the job done."

Tine didn't miss a beat. Laughing, he said, "Well, Sonny, if you and those nags get tired, you can load your itty bitty kittin' kaboodle on my wagon, and I'll git you where your goin'."

Infuriated, I turned and walked away.

It was like that throughout the entire trek. He would needle me every day. He took to calling me clodhopper as a derogatory way of saying I was a hick farmer. Remember, when plowing, you had to be nimble of foot walking on freshly turned soil. This was followed by childish pranks. I always hobble the horses at night. This consists of a piece of rope tied in a specific manner around their front legs so they can only take baby steps. It allowed them to range for food but not get too far from camp.

One morning, I went to gather the stock, and I found the hobble ropes on the ground and no horses. It was a real chore gathering them in, for they had literally wandered off to greener pastures. When I finally returned to camp with my charges, there was Tine twirling one of my hobble lines. "Clodhopper, don't you even know how to tie a rope?"

Frustrated and feeling like a small child being admonished, I muttered darkly, "Stay away from me and my rig."

"Or what?" Tine responded.

I walked away and said nothing more to him...for now!

9

"There never was a rougher set but jolly in their drink."
—Anonymous about wagoners

"For a whore is a deep ditch; and a strange woman is a narrow pit."
—Proverbs 23:27 (KJV)

Something was very wrong. Tine hadn't said a word, good or bad, all day long. In fact, he ignored me completely. This was more unsettling than his usual aggressive assaults on my person. We approached a newly opened establishment called Stuckey's Tavern. All the wagoners were excited about having a tavern meal instead of our own cooking and spending some time with ale and the six "sisters," supposedly Stuckey's "daughters" known as the Thatch Patch. Tine never said a word, but I was goaded by other drivers to participate with them in this special occasion.

Salivating at the thought of a good meal and wanting to impress my fellows that I was a man, not a boy, I readily assented to join them. After all, what harm could come from a hot meal and maybe even a single ale? We never consumed any alcoholic beverages on our farm—only spring water, milk, and tea for stimulation. I had a youthful inquisitiveness about alcohol. I had seen the effects of overconsumption but still wondered why so many people seemed to enjoy it. How did it taste? I would soon find out!

The tavern was a wooden two-story structure with a stone addition under construction. Inside, it had a very low ceiling that held smoke from the fireplace and tobacco smoke at eye level. Added to this haze was the unpleasant odor of unwashed bodies and bad breadth. There was a wooden floor rather than dirt, which was a rarity on the frontier. There was a second floor with bedrooms, where you could rent a sleeping place. The rooms were small and sparsely furnished. You didn't rent the room but rather a space on the bed, which was often shared with a stranger. Clean, fresh bedding cost extra.

A fiddler was playing the same merry tune over and over again. Some patrons danced with the "sisters," and some danced with each other. A few were gambling; but most were eating, drinking, and telling tall tales. I had never been in such a ruckus and noisy place in my life.

The meal, which composed venison stew and johnny cakes, was good; it was not as good as a home-cooked meal, but it was better than what we had been preparing for ourselves. Of course, everyone was drinking ale. At first, I declined to imbibe, even though I was sorely tempted. When Tine good-naturedly offered to pay for my drink, I accepted. Had I not been so inclined to really want to try an ale, I would have been suspicious; instead, I thought it a peace offering, and I accepted. Having no tolerance for alcohol, it didn't take long for me to get sloshed.

In my drunken state, I began noticing the Thatch Patch. Strange they didn't resemble each other at all! They had blonde, red, brown, and black hair. Some were dark-skinned while others were pale. They all wore a simple white cap on their heads barely concealing their abundant hair. They all wore a long blue skirt that swished seductively as they twirled around when serving tables and dancing. They wore a white cotton off-the-shoulder top that exposed arms, neck, chest and more than a little cleavage. I discovered they did not have good Christian names but rather were named after flowers. There was Rose, Lilly, Daisy, Iris, Impatience, and Astor. I remember thinking, *They should be called the flower patch.*

Feeling the effects of the ale, I lost my inhibitions—and my common sense—and succumbed to the wiles of the youngest sister named Astor. She had beautiful long black hair that tumbled down her shoulders when she removed her cap. Her skin was pale and smooth looking. She was not beautiful but not homely either. It was her smile that made her attractive. She flirted shamelessly and was soon sitting on my lap and nibbling on my ear. I was flattered. I thought she was attracted to my youth and good looks. Somebody (Tine, I think) gave her some money, and I was helped upstairs to a small private room barely large enough to accommodate a bed.

She was probably only a year or two older than me, but I was soon to learn she was vastly more experienced in sexual matters. She sat me on the edge of the bed and swayed her hips seductively in front of me. She would lean forward, overexposing more of her cleavage as she smiled and teased. When she fondled her own breasts, it pushed them up, exposing even more flesh. My body was not so inebriated that it didn't respond as any healthy young man would. Then she pulled her shoulder straps down, giving full exposure to her ample bosom. It was the most beautiful and seductive sight I had ever seen. I was so excited I was ready to burst.

Next, she came forward and pulled my face into her nakedness and rubbed their soft flesh all over my face. She smelled of a combination of brew, sweat, and lavender; and in my state, it was an elixir of love and lust. She pushed me down on the bed and uncinched my breeches, exposing my excited manhood. Her face lit up, and she exclaimed, "It's beautiful!" Not a word I would have used to describe it. She then raised her skirt over her hips, exposing her womanhood. Thatch patch indeed! She rose over me. It was all over in seconds. Not minutes—seconds. To me, the sweet release was *geweldig* (wonderful)!

I awoke the next morning in my bedroll and a puddle of venison stew and ale vomit. I had a terrible hangover, and my aching head winced at the screeching laughter and ridicule piercing my ears. It was Tine. Through his laughter, he was saying, "Well, Clodhopper, guess you ain't so high and mighty now! No, sir, you ain't the goody-goody you let on. Now you're a sinner just like the rest of us."

It was all beginning to make some sense now—he set me up! He wanted to bring me down from what he thought was my high perch and was even willing to pay coin to do it. I was as angry as I had ever been. I stumbled toward him, my hands in a fist and in a fit of rage, reverted to Pennsylvania Dutch, shouting repeatedly, "*Klootzok* [bas-

tard]! *Der geilsmischt* [horse shit]! *Der kinkelmischt* [chicken shit]!"
Tine didn't understand what I was saying, but he knew it wasn't good.

I saw real fear in his beady eyes as he saw rage in mine. Two
other wagoners held me in restraint or maybe also holding me up. I
was in pretty bad shape. They took me to a nearby creek and threw
me in to cool my temper. It actually felt refreshing and revived me
somewhat. It had the other benefit of washing the vomit off of me,
but it did nothing to soothe my anger, and I vowed to get even.

10

"Part of the study of history involves a training of the imagination, learning to see historical actors as speaking and acting in their own times rather than ours; and learning to see even our heroes as an all-to-human mixture of admirable and unadmirable qualities, people like us who may, like us, be constrained by circumstances beyond their control…"
—Wilfred M. McClay (historian)

I was bitter and angry. I wanted revenge! Tine avoided me; in fact, *everyone* avoided me. I was treated like a leper. All the drivers thought I should be grateful for the "good time" I had. They could not comprehend me and my background. To them, it was all in good fun. Truth is in my misery, I was not a fit person to be around.

As we traveled, I plotted my revenge. Some of the plots were very childish. I considered keeping the fish guts from one of our freshly caught suppers and stashing them in Tine's wagon. I could image the horrible smell that would attract vermin and the maggots that would be crawling all through his wagon bed and his cargo. It would take him days to figure it out. The thought of it made me smile, but it did not ease my pain. In the end, I did not execute any of my schemes.

Even in my rage, I could not escape my family background and religious training. I reflected on that moment of pleasure and how it had cost me a lot. I had taken a big fall in one night. I not only committed drunkenness and fornication, but I had also added bitterness and unforgiveness to the list of sins. If all of that was not bad enough, I had also set a horrible example as a professing Christian. Ma always said, "It is not enough to know your faith. You must also live it."

It didn't happen all at once, but gradually I realized my anger was not directed at Tine. I was really upset with *myself*. I could—and did—make excuses. I was young. I was set up. I was taken advantage of…but I willingly went into a situation I sensed was wrong and then compounded it. Ma also said the first step to correcting a problem was to recognize it. I recognized the problem, and it was me. So I did nothing to Tine; but I must admit I still enjoyed seeing him on edge, wondering how and when I would exact the revenge that would never come from me. As I pondered on Tine, it made me realize that I did not want to be like him—an unhappy, friendless, faithless sad sack.

As I lost interest in revenge, my thoughts turned to sex—not the act itself but rather the implications of the act. Pa never explained about sex as a physical act, for he knew we saw livestock engaging in procreation all the time on the farm. What he did say was carnal feasting out of wedlock leads to sin, death, and destruction. It weakens faith. You can get a very uncomfortable and even life-threatening disease from it. And if pregnancy results, you can wind up in a loveless marriage.

To me, this was all scary stuff. I knew I had sinned, but had I contracted a disease? I checked myself often for a long time. Worse, what if Astor was pregnant? I was haunted by these questions, and they weighed on me much as my impending revenge weighed on Tine. Indeed, that was a very costly night.

To squelch these uncomfortable thoughts, I reminisced about home. I smiled as I remembered Solomon—not the king but the ram. We had about two dozen sheep on the farm; and our one and only ram was Solomon, named after the biblical king that had 700 wives and 300 concubines. Sheep usually meander independently around a pasture while grazing and only flock together when facing danger, like a dog attack. I was the one who saw the clustered flock and went to check on them. Turned out that it wasn't danger that brought them together. It was procreation.

Most of the ewes had come into heat at the same time, and they were all hanging around Solomon to be bred. He was servicing them all, and it had taken its toll. His head was down, his tongue was lolling out of his mouth, he was breathing heavily, and he looked like he had lost twenty pounds. I led him back to the paddock and grained and watered him, but it was too late. He lay down and died, but he did die with a smile on his lips. One hundred and fifty-two days later, we had thirty-two lambs born. I thought of my own pathetic sexual encounter and the toll it had taken on me. Maybe Solomon the ram was a king after all?

11

"A house is not a home unless it contains food
and fire for the mind as well as the body."
—Benjamin Franklin

Alone. I never felt so alone. I was homesick. I felt a dull ache in my heart and my stomach. This was the first time I had ever been away from home, and things were not going well. I missed my family, the farm, and my normal routine and way of life. I wanted—I needed—someone to tell me everything was going to be all right. I thought I would enjoy the freedom of making my own decisions; but now I yearned for someone to guide me, to tell me what to do.

As I traveled, I spent more time reminiscing about home. In my mind, I could smell Ma's cooking and hear Henry's adulation. To a lesser extent, I even missed Jacob's taunts. I missed the beauty of Kreutz Creek Valley, Sunday church, and all the community events that brought joy to hard work. We would gather together to share the burdens of butter boiling, wheat harvesting, apple cider making, and corn husking.

This day, I was thinking about a particular corn husking event last October 1754. Corn husking is hard work. Tearing the husks off the ear of corn took strength and wreaked havoc on the hands. To make this boring, difficult task more acceptable, the young folk—male and female—were paired; each had his/her "partner," and by custom, the finding of a red ear entitled the lucky finder to a kiss from his fair one. Though by custom as well, it was ever the result of easy conquest at the end of a short and faintly contested "show battle," often while the light was extinguished.

My partner was Sarah Kauffman. She had smiled and flirted with me at church, so I figured our interests were mutually shared (in other words, I think she liked me). We were all laughing and enjoying ourselves when Sarah thrust an ear of corn into my hands—it was a red ear! Upon seeing this, everyone oohed and aahed, and the light was blown out. Sarah took the initiative. She looked at me coyly, and without any fake resistance or fanfare, she kissed me!

I was remembering now the thrill of that kiss. Her lips were soft, warm, and moist; and I felt a jolt go through my body. I wished that kiss would have lasted forever. It was *geweldig*! After that, all I would dream about was Sarah and I getting married and having a life together. In my current loneliness, I yearned to see her again.

Sarah was a few months older than me, and she was beautiful. Like me, she was tall for her age, and she was also tall for a girl; but she carried herself with such grace that her height was not intimidating. I knew that under her cap, there was a full head of gorgeous brown hair. Her skin tone was slightly tanned from time outdoors, in the sun. Her brown eyes sparkled under pretty lush eyebrows. Her nose was in perfect proportion to her face. Her mouth always seemed to be in a smile, showing off her perfect teeth and those wonderful sensuous lips I wanted to kiss again and again!

Suddenly, Astor came to mind, and I felt ashamed. I thought my sins so terrible that God wouldn't forgive me, but at that moment, I realized from my training that Jesus died for *all* sins—even mine. Right then I asked God for forgiveness and help, and a tremendous weight was lifted from me. I also determined no one needed to know of my downfall. It was between God and myself.

With that burden removed, my thoughts turned to sex again. You might think that is quite a leap from God to sex, but I was trying to look at it from his perspective. I was thinking of sex in marriage with Sarah. *Is this what the Bible means when it talks of marriage resulting in "one flesh"?* I considered this for quite a while; then I thought of Ma and Pa.

It is hard to think of your parents ever having intercourse, but of course, they do. I was living proof of that. But my thoughts went beyond the physical. Ma and Pa shared faith, dreams, goals, hard work, joys, and sorrows. I realized there are many kinds of intimacy in marriage. They shared body, mind, heart, and soul with each other. They worked as one—"one flesh"! This is what I wanted! I wanted to share *everything* with Sarah.

As I pondered all of these things, my spirit lifted, and I began to feel like my old self. I had weathered a personal storm, and I hoped I came out of it a better person. I was still homesick but, I felt right with God and had hope of a future with Sarah. Sarah Herbach. That sounded mighty good to me.

I felt like I had a new lease on life. I was once again noticing and enjoying the wonders of God's creation around me. Turkeys were everywhere, and they seemed unafraid of our presence. Tom turkeys were gobbling, so they had their minds on mating rather than caution. A lone mockingbird serenaded us all night long; he never seemed to tire. The Juniata River was full of fish. We ate lots of catfish, bass, and sunfish as we followed its banks to the small village of Raystown.

John McCray built a tavern here in 1751, and other trades and homes soon appeared around it. I thought the river and the countryside around it beautiful, and judging from the limestone outcropping, I saw it to be fertile. I felt good enough, secure enough, to enjoy a meal at the inn; but I had no alcohol. The nature of the place was much different than Stuckey's. It was much less bawdy, and there were no "sisters."

We were warned by the locals that the Shawnee Indians often camped at a place about ten miles west of town called Shawnee Cabins. It was a temporary campsite used by the Indians when hunting or raiding in the area. They migrated from their home base in "Ken-tuck-ee" in search of game. They particularly sought the numerous deer and *mkwa* (bear) in the area. Unfortunately, they sometimes were hostile and hunted men!

Their last visit to the region was not a friendly one—they killed several workers on the Burd Road crew. One particularly sage woodsman said not to worry, for all the hostiles were moving to join the French and their Indian allies at Fort Duquesne. We proceeded south, along Wills Mountain, with caution but saw no sign of savages as we moved toward Fort Cumberland (formerly Wills Creek).

I could see why the Indians hunted *mkwa* in this place; there was bear scat everywhere. The woods looked like a pasture just grazed by a herd of cows. I saw one mama bear with four cubs. I never knew they could birth and raise so many cubs. I kept at a distance because I did not want to appear to be a threat to them; she bears can be very nasty and aggressive to protect their young. I chuckled to myself as I watched the bear family antics happening before me. Poor mama bear was constantly busy, keeping her brood corralled.

One cub in particular seemed to want to do his own thing, dashing here and there, disobeying his mother's commands. Mother bear had the harried look I had seen in human mothers when dealing with their children. After they had passed, I continued my hunt for food, for our supper.

I heard a lone musket shot. My first thought was it was an Indian attack. I crouched in an alert position, musket ready. Then I heard a frantic hollering in a high pitch, "HELP, HELP, HELP!" Into a clearing burst Tine, his skinny stick legs moving faster than I ever could have imagined. Right behind him was an angry black bear, teeth barred as it closed in on Tine. I instinctively raised my weapon, aimed, and pulled the trigger. The bear stopped in its tracks, looked at me, took two steps toward me, and then tumbled over.

Tine, hands on his knees and trying to catch his breath, squeaked out a weak "Thanks." I figured he shot at the bear, wounding but not killing it. I hoped it wasn't the mama bear with the four cubs.

"Why would you shoot a bear when we have no way to preserve all the meat? Such a waste! Don't thank me. I couldn't decide if I wanted to shoot you or the bear. The bear was already wounded, and we can eat the bear meat. You, on the other hand, aren't worth wasting lead on!"

That night, we had bear steaks and rendered the lard to grease our wagon axles. Other than the bear incident, the rest of this leg of the trip was uneventful, and I continued to ignore Tine.

12

"[It] is situated within two hundred yards of Wills Creek, on a hill and about four hundred from the Potomack; its length from east to west is about 200 yards, and breadth 46 yards, and is built by logs driven into the ground, and about twelve feet above it."

—British Officer

We could hear Fort Cumberland long before we saw it. The sounds of hammers clanging on anvils and driving nails into wood, the swishing sound of saws cutting timber, drums rolling, and troops marching, livestock of all sorts bellowing, and people hollering and barking orders were heard a half-hour before we arrived. The smells assaulted our senses as well. We went from the wonderful odors of forests and field to the acrid smell of smoke from many fires and the pungent and disgusting odor of animal and human waste.

As we got closer, I caught a whiff of a more pleasant scent. With my huge appetite, I was keenly aware of anything related to food and was able to sort out the smell of bread baking. In this solitary instance, the stomach ruled over the nose! I later discovered that due to a lack of ovens, the bread was baked in holes in the ground, resulting in gritty bread, containing sand and dirt.

It was amazing to me to see this small city in the midst of the wilderness. There were thousands of soldiers, carpenters, blacksmiths, road builders, wagoners, and camp followers. Plus, there were horses and livestock in the midst of the fort and the hundreds of ramshackle shacks, tents and wagons around it. It was like a mountain metropolis and I was impressed.

As we arrived, our little group of some two dozen wagons was greeted by a British officer who informed us we were now under the command of the British army. So despite Mr. Franklin's assurances of independence, we discovered we would be subject to British military discipline and order. General Braddock had appointed a "wagon master general" and deputies to oversee us. Each deputy had forty wagons under his command and was responsible for enforcing the rules. We were warned that if any of the rules were disobeyed, we "would be punished according to our just desserts."

The rules included "mustering"—that is, gathering for inspection our horses every morning and evening as if they were soldiers. The reason for this was horses were so valuable that they were being stolen. They were actually under guard. We were also assigned an order of march each day. Failure to respond to any orders could result in "disciplinary action." I was assigned to my group of forty wagons and, once again, would have a new set of traveling companions.

My parting with Tine Elliot had an odd twist to it. As usual, Tine was all puffed up about how superior his wagon and horses were compared to our "farm" wagons. As an officer approached to give him his assignment, he expected praise; but instead the officer told him to pull out of line—his services were not needed! His beady eyes bulged out of his head in disbelief. What was wrong? It was explained to him that experience had already shown the army that big wagons were a deterrent in the wild frontier environment of an army road. They told him he might get work hauling supplies from Frederick or Winchester to Fort Cumberland; but his contract, with its provisions for replacement value, were null and void.

Tine stammered and stuttered in disbelief and tried to argue his case—to no avail. The officer, tiring of Tine's blubbering, threatened, "We need horses, and yours look very fit. Maybe we should commandeer them?" Tine was so taken aback that his stogie fell from his lips. I had never seen him without that thing in his mouth; in fact, I was beginning to believe he slept with it in his mouth! The thought of losing his "matched" team of horses struck him to his very core. He may have been a despicable human being, but he did love and take good care of his horses.

At that moment, I actually felt sorry for him. I thought back to my Bible study lessons; and somewhere in Thessalonians, it says something like, "God is just. He will pay back trouble to those that trouble you." Ashamed and embarrassed, Tine sheepishly led his team away. I would never have contact with him again. I guess with God's help, the "clodhopper" got his justice.

13

"A friend is someone who understands your past, believes
in your future, and accepts you just the way you are."

—Unknown

I assumed my new place in the wagon line and then went to get my
army ration of food. My food supply from home was long gone; and
I had subsisted on game killed along the route, mostly turkey. My
stomach growled as I gathered my watered-down "mystery stew" and
some bread.

I was looking for a place to sit and eat when a voice with a thick
Irish accent said, "Here's a place."

I accepted the offer and found myself seated next to redheaded
boy in a British uniform.

"Ye be a bit young fer a driver?"

I responded, "And you are awfully young to be a soldier."

We both smiled and extended our hands to shake.

"I be Tim Murphy, and I am a drummer," he said with pride.

"I'm Jost Herbach, and I am not only a driver—but a good
one—and an even better farmer!"

We both laughed. I liked this boy right off the bat, and by his
warm smile, I could tell the feeling was mutual.

"So," I said, "I can tell you take pride in being a drummer.
What are your duties as a drummer?"

"'Tis a very responsible job. Soldiers not only march to my beat,
but they understand the talkin' of the drum. They know what beat
sounds assembly or advance or retreat or parlay. The whole army
knows my drums!"

"I had no idea what is involved in being a drummer. I am very impressed. How did you learn all of this?"

"Me whole life—all twelve years of it—has been spent in the army. I never knew me Dadai. He died before I could remember him. Mamai said he was a corporal in the 44th Foot and very brave. He died in the battle of Prestonpans in 1745, fighting against the Jacobites. Mamai was a laundress and continued her labor until her death over a year ago of camp disease. So being an orphan, the army made me a drummer. Bein' around the army all the time, I already knew the beats."

"So you are all alone?" I was now thinking of my own loneliness.

As he stretched out his arms in a sweeping motion over all around us, he said, "Nay, I have all me mates."

I thought, *I will never take my family for granted ever again!*

"How'd a farmer become a driver?"

I told him about meeting Benjamin Franklin and how Pa chose me over Jacob to be responsible for the horses and wagons. I may have inflated my importance to impress him. Next, he asked about farming.

"Farming is hard work, but there are many rewards. I often have a sense of accomplishment, of getting things done. It is an exhilarating feeling to look back on a freshly plowed field or to see grain sprouting or bringing in a big harvest. Work changes according to the season or even the time of day."

Tim's eyes sparkled. "I hope to own land and have me self a family someday—a real family. A wife and young'uns. Tell me more about the farm and your family."

I told him about my nemesis, Jacob; my admirer, Henry; Ma and Pa; Tauser; church; and…well…everything. It made me feel important that he hung on every word I said. It was plain to see—he wanted what I had, and again I was thankful for the life I had been given by God. It dawned on me that Tim was my new Henry. It was always nice to be looked up to.

He slapped his knee and said, "Come on. I'll show you around the fort. I can also fix ya up with a sprightly maid if you like!"

I accepted the invitation to see more of my temporary new home but declined the offer for feminine companionship. As we walked, I told him about Astor; and he wondered why I was so upset; after all, women were there for the pleasure of men. I guess this was a soldier's point of view. I went on to tell him about Sarah and my plans for a good Christian family. As I explained more, he thought Sarah sounded like the perfect partner to be—just what he would want for himself.

We spent much time together, telling stories and sharing dreams. I enjoyed watching the troop's drill, and Tim was proud of my interest in his way of life. I had very little contact with the military, except for seeing a few soldiers in town. But now, here in front of me was a whole regiment going through their drills, and I was impressed. They wore their regimental red coats with bright-yellow cuffs and fringes. Their white gaiters buttoned up tightly revealing their calve contours. They wore polished black shoes. A waist belt held up their britches and had a leather bayonet holder. They also wore a cartridge pouch with a large buff leather strap.

Each soldier was armed with a musket, bayonet, a small sword known as a "hanger," and 24 cartridges in the pouch. The head gear was a tricorn hat bound with lace turned up on three sides and known as a cocked hat. To me, they made a formidable appearance. The men, who the night before seemed like nothing but a group of drunken ruffians, now marched as one unit; and they were crisp and sharp in their movements.

In my youthful ignorance, I almost envied Tim. What an adventure it would be to be part of such a grand force! When I thought no one was looking, I followed their lead and would practice snapping to attention and briskly saluting. I was truly impressed and could not imagine anything standing against this force. When I wasn't spending time with Tim, I made some new friends among the wagoners; and this time, they were mostly commendable and friendly men.

14

"I can't say as ever I was lost, but I was
bewildered once for three days."

—Daniel Boone

"Friendship is born at the moment one person
says to another, 'What! You too?
I thought I was the only one.'"

—C.S. Lewis

May–June 1755

I enjoyed my time with Tim immensely, but we each had our duties to attend to—his with the army and mine with the care and maintenance of my team. Horses needed to be fed and groomed, and harnesses and gear needed to be cleaned and axles greased. As I did these chores, I tended to avoid interaction with my fellow wagoners; after all, my experiences with them had not been the best. I did notice a rather rough fellow by the name of Dan Morgan, who was head of the line and in front of me. A cheerful young man by the name of Daniel Boone was behind me. Down the line was John Finely, Matt Laird, and some of the men from my old convoy.

It was Daniel Boone that broke the ice. He approached me with a bright smile and extended hand. "I am Daniel Boone, and I think it best we get to know one another as we will be traveling together."

I was only momentarily rattled by his approach as his smile put me at ease.

With a firm handshake, I introduced myself. "My name is Jost. Jost Herbach. And I come from Kreutz Creek Valley in the newly formed York County, Pennsylvania."

"Small world! I was born and raised in Berks County, near Reading, Pennsylvania. If you tell me you're from a farming family, I'll think we may have a lot in common." And we did, but it was more than just farming!

We quickly discovered we both shared a deep religious faith. I was a member of the German Reformed Lutheran Church. He was raised a Quaker, but his family was disavowed by his church when first his brother and later his sister married non-Quakers ("marrying out"). Though officially, he was no longer a Quaker, I could see in him a gentleness and kindness that went with being raised a pacifist. We both loved the Lord, and this created an immediate bond between us. As time went on, we would pray together. How different from old Tine Elliot...

Reading was another activity we shared. In fact, he had two books with him: the Bible, which he read daily, and *Gulliver's Travels* by Jonathon Swift. He honored me by letting me borrow these books. It felt good to have a Bible in my hands again, but the real revelation was *Gulliver's Travels*. I had never read a book like it, and it fascinated me. Imagine the adventure of giants and little people! As I read it, I realized why Daniel had it—it was a traveler's tale, and at heart, Daniel was a traveler.

He was around twenty-one years of age but seemed vastly more experienced in the ways of the world than that. He was my height but with a broader, slightly heavy build. He kept his reddish-brown, almost sandy hair tied under the broad brimmed hat he wore. He had fair skin and a somewhat Roman nose. His countenance was such that he made friends easily, including me!

He asked my age, and when I told him I was fourteen years old, he lightly slapped my back and said, "You're a biggin' and on a grand experience like this. I remember when I was your age, I killed my first bear!"

I noticed he said *first*, so there must have been others.

He continued, "My Pa gave me my first firearm when I was twelve years old, and I spent every free moment of time hunting the woods around the farm. Pa encouraged me because I always brought home a meal. Over the years, I've kilt many deer, elk, and even bison both in Berks County and in the Yadkin River area of North Carolina, where I call home these days. Why, I've shot so much game that I can shoot a tick off the bear's nose! That's why I call this here rifle Old Tick Licker."

"How did you kill your bear?" I asked.

"Well, he just came running at me. I didn't have time to even think. I just pulled my gun up and shot him dead!"

"Wait a minute. You said *your*. Did you kill a bear too?"

"As a matter of fact, I did."

I told him my story of shooting a bear to save old Tine Elliot.

He was impressed. "If you ain't full of surprises!"

It was just another thing we had in common. Over the course of the next few weeks, I would hear many stories of his hunts. Certainly hunting, not farming, was his real passion.

Daniel had the courtesy to ask me about my hunting experiences.

"I love hunting the hills around our farm—mostly small game. The biggest critter I ever shot there was a big old white-tailed deer buck, but my favorite hunting is for waterfowl on the Susquehanna River. We used the Indian practice of 'sneak hunting,' or as we called it 'sneak boating'."

Daniel sounded almost incredulous. "Sneak boating? I've done a lot of hunting, but what is that?"

"First off," I replied, "during fall migration, there are thousands and thousands of waterfowl that fly from north to south along the river. There are mallards, black ducks, teals, canvasbacks, redheads, geese, swans, and many others. They sometimes darken the sky with their numbers. Following the practice of the local Indians, we would tie brush to our boats to make them look like floating debris. Early in the morning, before daylight, we would quietly slip the boat into the water. As daylight approached, we would lay in the bottom of the boat. It was hard and uncomfortable and most often, teeth-chattering cold.

"We would drift with the current toward the resting and feeding birds. When close enough for a good shot, we would sit up and fire with our scatterguns as the frightened birds lifted off the water. At that point, they were level with our guns, and we would get two or more birds per shot. We would retrieve our kills and repeat the process till the waterfowl became suspicious or continued their trek south. We collected thirty or more birds each trip in this manner."

"Well, I'll be! Ain't that somethin'! I gotta try that someday."

I could see the admiration in his eyes. That I was able to impress this natural-born hunter with my story made me feel somewhat akin to him, and it felt good.

I replied, "You know I am more than just another pretty face!"

We had a good laugh over that. Other hunting and fishing stories would be told over the coming weeks. We also discovered other things we had in common. He was the sixth of ten children, and I was the fourth of seven. He talked about his wife, Rebecca, whom he had married in North Carolina. Of course, I shared my dream of a life with Sarah. Unusual for the time, he did not use tobacco, and neither did I. He did drink alcohol but never to excess.

It was Daniel who introduced me formally to Dan Morgan and John Finely.

15

"All you need for happiness is a good gun,
a good horse and a good wife."
—Daniel Boone

"Nature was here [Kentucky] a series of
wonders and a fund of delight."
—Daniel Boone

I felt like I had to drop to my knees, for the handshake was a vice like grip. On the other end of the extended hand was Dan Morgan. Daniel (Boone) introduced him as his cousin and me to him as his friend. Dan (Morgan) was not trying to intimidate through his grip; he was just naturally so strong that the strength surged through his arm into his handshake. He was tall—six feet, two inches—and broad and muscular. Even at his young age of twenty-one years, he had a slightly receding hairline. His face was deeply tanned, and he sported a scar over his forehead. His prominent Roman nose was set between friendly brown eyes that could turn black and dangerous in an instant. He was a formidable and imposing presence.

I was next introduced to a tall, lanky balding man, who looked to be some forty years of age. I shook hands with John Finely. A trader and a hunter like Daniel, he had a host of hunting stories, but his obsession was "Ken-tuck-ee." He never tired of telling the wonders of that land west of the Appalachian Mountains.

"The woods have so much game you don't need to go after it when hunting. You just sit a little, and it will come to you! Deer, elk, bear, bison… Small game too! Rabbits, squirrels, grouse, turkey—the abundance is overwhelming! The bison are so numerous they migrate from one grass meadow to the next. They make what I call Bison Roads through the forests, trampling brush and even small trees into the ground. They grow to huge sizes feeding on the beautiful lush grasses I call 'bluegrass' because their flower heads are blue.

"These meadows stretch for miles. The land is so fertile that even after being trampled and grazed by the herds, it recovers new growth quickly. Of course, it is well fertilized by those same herds. Sometimes it takes a whole day for a herd to pass by. Ain't nothin' like it! Why, a blind man could hunt there and live well!"

His favorite story was about being captured by the Shawnee Indians. They must have been the same Shawnee we had been warned about in Raystown.

"I was sittin', quietly taking in the beauty of the countryside, when the sudden quietness seemed amiss. I hunkered down in a sweet-smelling honeysuckle bush. Sure enough, after a few minutes, a small group of Indians came by at about fifty yards distance. I stayed hid for ten minutes after they passed and was just congratulating myself on avoiding detection when I felt the cold muzzle of a musket pressed against my skull.

"How could I have been caught so off guard? I was roughly pushed to the ground and forced to strip naked. My hands were bound with leather straps, and a leather leash was tied around my neck. They weren't in their war paint, but they still looked mighty fearsome. My mind whirled with thoughts of horrible tortures and my coming demise."

He had my full attention. I knew he lived to tell the story because he was doing just that. Tim was with us that evening, and his eyes were as big as a hoot owl's. The two Dans had heard the story before, many times, but listened with attention and serious smiles on their faces.

"I understood Shawnee talk, so I was shocked as they talked about how they found me. They *smelled* me, even hidden in honeysuckle! They laughed how easy it was to sneak right up on top of me. They called me a fool and simple minded—and maybe I was—but I decided to play along as a crazy person. It just might save my life. We went on a forced march, taking several days, back to their village.

"Being naked and shoeless, I became covered with cuts, scratches, and bruises but knew if I stopped or faltered, I would be kilt. When we finally arrived, the squaws and children greeted me with taunts, spit, and pointed sticks. And didn't those bastards aim those sticks at my private parts! Even their cur dogs nipped at me. They tied my leash to a pole and left me to agonize about my fate. Playin' the fool must have helped because they eventually eased their attacks.

"Bye and bye, they threw me some gnarly, nasty meat, which I greedily ate. They also gave me my clothes back. They weren't much, all torn and tattered, so no one else would have wanted them. After a few days, they untied me and allowed me the freedom to walk around the village. They thought I was harmless, and it was considered bad luck to harm a crazy person. After another day, they told me to leave, and I didn't waste any time gittin' out of there. The more I thought about it, I decided they cut me loose because I was bald—no scalp worth takin'. Anyway, here I am to tell about it, so I ain't too much a fool."

I was impressed, and so was Tim. I was impressed, not only by the story but also by the way it was told. It was apparent that storytelling was an important part of being a wagoner. I was learning to be attentive while listening and to embellish when telling a yarn. A good storyteller made fun of himself but always persevered in the end. John had told this story many times. I would hear it again; but it still had a freshness, a sincerity about it each time. One thing I was sure of, I liked him.

16

"Those Wagoners are the most irregular set of
People that I have ever had to do with."

—British Officer

May 1755

Old Dan Morgan was somewhat of a contradiction. He wasn't old
(twenty-one years), yet he called himself old. His transport business
(he was a wagoner) was called Old Dan Morgan. He had the repu-
tation of being a "coarse jester," a gambler, and a heavy drinker; but
he was most noted for being a brawler. This was akin to being a professional fighter. Brawling was brutal with *anything* being allowed,
except deadly weapons and killing. Gouging eyes, biting ears and
nose, kicking anywhere (ribs, groin, head), breaking bones (nose,
fingers, arms, legs), were all permitted. Old Dan was respected and
feared for his fighting skills.

He told us how he had run away from home when he was six-
teen and wandered through Pennsylvania to Carlisle, then south to
Winchester, Virginia. His first employment was clearing forestland
for agricultural use. Since he was paid by the acre and not by the
hour, he worked from morning into dark swinging an axe and moving rocks. It was this work that developed his huge muscles and giant
calloused hands and fists that would demolish his fighting opponents.

His employer admired his work ethic and his native intelligence
and soon promoted him to supervisor of a sawmill. A customer of the
mill saw those same characteristics and his toughness and hired him
as a wagoner. Soon, the enterprising Old Dan prospered and owned
his own wagon and team. All this happened in just four years.

When he told stories about his fights, he would stand dancing around and jabbing with his fists as if his opponent was in front of him. In typical wagoner fashion, he would make noises to accompany his tale: *bam*, snap, thud, smack, crunch, *yeow, oof, aagh,* crack, groan, rip. As he spoke, his hands and arms moved in and out so fast they were a blur. He was not only amazingly strong but also quick and agile. The more I got to know him, it was apparent he was also intelligent. Put it all together, and this was a tough combination for anyone to defeat in combat.

I briefly witnessed his fighting skill in action. Tim came running and hollering, "There's going to be a fight. A big brute of an Irish soldier cheated Old Dan at cards. Better hurry!" Till we got there, the fisticuffs had already begun. We saw Old Dan step aside as a giant of a man dove for him. As the unbalanced soldier passed by, Old Dan gave him a vicious kick to the rump.

While the staggering soldier tried to regain his footing, Dan smashed a huge fist into his face. We could hear the nose break from the impact. Blood gushed from his broken nose as he fell to the ground, out cold. As we walked with Dan back to our wagons, he was limping; he had broken his big toe when he kicked his foe. That sore toe would give him problems over the next few weeks.

I soon discovered another side to this complex man. Yes, he drank alcohol, but I never saw him drunk. Yes, he liked gaming, but he knew when to quit. And yes, he was coarse but no more so than most wagoners and the British soldiers. For all his brutality, I also saw him show compassion, including to me and Tim. He despised any injustice but was particularly opposed to the British disciplinary custom of flogging—whipping the bare back and buttocks of victims, ripping off skin, and exposing raw flesh and even bone.

He really disliked all authority, and the British army was a symbol for all authority. Dan had grit, determination, loyalty to friends, competitiveness, and willingness to learn along with his aforementioned work ethic. He was a natural leader and attracted a following. He was a man's man!

As I look back and reflect upon the strange collection of men and boys assembled, I marvel at the bond we formed in such a short time. A twelve-year-old army drummer, a fourteen-year-old German farmer, a twenty-one-year-old hunter, a twenty-one-year-old wagoner, and a forty-something peddler and dreamer—what a diverse assembly! Not only did I personally learn much from this cast of characters, but I also realize now we supported each other's needs. Tim needed a father figure, and now he had several. Old Dan was rough, but he had a good heart and as a sixteen-year-old runaway felt a kinship with an orphan and a young man on his first adventure away from home for the first time.

Daniel and I were the only believers, but as we read our Bible and spoke of matters of faith, I could see the others listening and seeking God, especially Old Dan. Ma always said God is good and that he works in mysterious ways. I realized I was living it. I know I also learned how to tell a story and a little about fighting. (Watch out, Jacob!)

17

"They loved to talk of Washington-
His virtues and his noble deeds
In war and peace; and whose renown,
More brilliant than the royal crown
No panegyrics needs-
Whose brilliant example will outlive
All honors titled names could give."

—H. L. Fisher

Tim had a little time off and was visiting with me. An officer on horseback approached, and Tim snapped to attention and saluted. Since I had been practicing saluting on my own, I instinctively did likewise. The officer gave a routine return salute, but he was momentarily startled when he realized I was not a soldier but a young wagoner. The slightest grin, not near enough to call a smile, was shown on his tight-lipped mouth as he passed by.

The startled officer was none other than the second most famous man in the colonies (after Benjamin Franklin), Colonel George Washington, the aide-de-camp to General Braddock. His accounts of his exploits on the frontier were published in every paper in the colonies and in England and were well known to everyone. He traveled in the Ohio country as a surveyor at age seventeen.

In 1753, he carried a letter from Governor Dinwiddie of Virginia demanding the French to immediately vacate the area claimed by the Crown and Virginia. On his return trip, he traversed nine hundred miles, including hiking through snowy woods and falling off a raft into the Allegheny River, nearly drowning. He spent a freezing night on an island without shelter and for all of this, came to no harm.

Within a few months, he was commissioned a Lt. Colonel in command of 150 men to evict the intruding French. He came upon a small force and, engaging them, killed ten Frenchmen, including their commander. He was pursued by a much larger force of French and their Indian allies and was forced to hastily assemble a defensive palisade he named Fort Necessity. After a short battle, with heavy losses, he surrendered the fort after signing a document written in French which stated he was the cause of the conflict. He marched out of Fort Necessity with colors flying and returned to Virginia.

His report of these events was much more descriptive than this summary. People were impressed with his trials and tribulations and on confronting the despised French with a small victory than they were with his ultimate defeat. He was a hero throughout the colonies. I recall reading his exploits; and now, after hearing all these wagoners stories, I concluded he could be made an honorary wagoner just on his storytelling abilities alone. After this, every time I saw the colonel, I would give him a crisp salute; and he would reply in kind, along with the smirk on his lips.

He had a presence about him well beyond his reported age of twenty-one years. He rode straight and tall, almost stiff backed on his mount. Dismounted he stood six feet and two inches tall, and his air was that of a self-assured young man. I was beginning to wonder if there was something special about being a big man since so many of my recent acquaintances were tall and leaders of men.

One evening, our little group was enjoying some general conversation.

Daniel asked John, "Why do you and others call the Frenchies frogs?"

"Did you ever hear them fellas talk? It sounds like a damn frog croaking—that's why." Then he made a series of odd noises imitating the French. "*Rrrrp, rrrp…Ribbet, ribbet…Burup, burup!*" We all laughed heartily.

Old Dan chimed in, "Naw, it's because frogs is their favorite meal!"

"Really?" I asked.

"Well, what do they call you Germans?"

After a little thought, I responded, "Krauts."

"Why is that?"

"I guess it's because we eat sauerkraut."

"There you go! It's because of what you eat! Why do they call the British *Rosbifs*?"

"I don't know. Why do they?"

"It's simple. It's because they eat roast beef!"

We all had a good laugh and the subject turned to fishing. I was in my element here telling of the huge sturgeon in the Susquehanna River, and the eel runs up the river and even into our little Kreutz Creek. What really caught their attention was the fish tale about the huge shad and herring runs up the river in the spring.

"Their numbers are so thick that you could walk across the river on their backs. The Indians made fish traps out of brush to enclose and capture the fish. We use nets to do the same thing. We salt them in barrels by the thousands."

"I would like to hear more about these shad."

The voice out of the darkness startled us all. Then out of the shadows stepped Colonel Washington. We all started to rise, and Tim and I stood at attention.

"Relax. This visit is personal and not official. I could not help but overhear your conversation. My home, Mount Vernon, is located on the Potomac River, and we also have these shad runs. I am very interested in turning those fish into profit. I understand there is a huge demand in Europe for these fish and their roe."

We introduced ourselves all around, and I could see the admiration we all shared for this young man, even Old Dan. We talked further about when and how to harvest commercial amounts of this abundant resource. The colonel thanked us and assured us he would put this information to work on his estate. When we parted and said our "good evenings," he came to me and saluted. I gave him my very sharpest salute in return. Little did I realize that this chance meeting would lead to even closer encounters with this icon.

18

―――――――――

"We began our march, but surely such a one was never undertaken before... I apprehend [it] will be looked upon as Romantick by those who did not see, and therefore cannot comprehend, the difficulties of the march."
—Major William Sharpe, 48th Regiment, 1755

May–June 1755

Of course, we did more than sit around and tell stories. We were put to work making supply runs from Winchester. We hauled mostly food but also tools, ammunition, and fodder for the livestock. It seemed most of the food was consumed by the "city in the wilderness," as quickly as we delivered it. Whether due to carelessness or fraud, too often the food, mostly meat, was spoiled. We once hauled hogsheads of pork into camp that when opened, was rotten. The meat and brine had been placed in barrels made of green and uncured timber, which were not tight and leaked—the smell was awful. Even the meat that was deemed edible was barely so, being tough and very salty. Flour was often moldy and infested with weevils but was used anyway.

"It's called logistics!"

"Logistics? Never heard that word before. What does it mean?" I asked.

John answered, "It means making everything come together, making things work. Old happy face, Quartermaster General Saint Clair, has the job of bringing soldiers, horses, food, weapons, tools, wagons, artillery, tents, carpenters, road builders, blacksmiths—you name it—all together in some kind of orderly fashion so the army can advance and be assured of the supplies and support they need to win. It's a big, near-impossible job under these conditions."

I was somewhat impressed. If you'll recall, Saint Clair had supper at our farm and terrorized our community with his Prussian uniform and harsh manner. He was rude and obnoxious. At least now, I had some explanation for why he always looked like he had bitten into a sour apple. The few times our paths crossed at Fort Cumberland, he never gave any recognition to me for my family's hospitality, which was fine by me.

"I met the man back in York when he and Ben Franklin came to acquire wagons and horses. I didn't like him then, and I still don't, but I can see how that responsibility would weigh on a man."

Tim injected, "Then you'll be happy to know I overheard a conversation, where General Braddock seemed to be placing blame for the army's inability to advance on Saint Clair's shoulders. There were not enough horses and wagons, not enough food and supplies, and what we have is deficient. On top of that, he said there were not enough Indian allies, and the colonial troops are—sorry, fellas—'shoddy'!"

We all grunted at the shoddy remark, but we had come to expect it from the "superior" British.

Tim continued, "Despite all this adversity, the general said we are going to begin the advance tomorrow."

On the morning of May 29, 1755, Tim and the other drummers sounded assembly. There was an air of excitement, and finally, we were beginning the advance toward Fort Duquesne. The first contingent to move out consisted of 650 men. There were soldiers, laborers, engineers, sailors, miners, Indians, wheelwrights, blacksmiths, and us fifty wagons loaded with axes, whipsaws, shovels, block and tackle, barrels of blasting powder, spare parts for wagon repairs, medical supplies, and food. This initial advance had the difficult task of making a road passable for the rest of the army and artillery to navigate.

We were following the very rough frontier road used by Col. Washington when he led his expedition to evict the French from the Ohio country. There is a big difference between a frontier road and a military road. It was more like a path than a road and required widening and removal of rocks and trees to accommodate heavy artillery and wagons.

What had started with some fanfare soon became a series of fits and starts. Every one hundred yards or so, we would have to stop and wait while crews worked on the road. Our first major obstacle was at a place called Sandy Gap, on Haystack Mountain, which was an almost perpendicular rock cliff. The sailors who were included in the expedition for their talents in water travel, it was hoped that some travel would be by water, and using block and tackle, they rigged systems to lift/lower wagons up/down the mountains. It was a disaster, with wagons blowing in the wind and crashing into the cliffs. Three wagons were completely destroyed and others badly damaged.

One of the latter included Old Dan Morgan's wagon, and we were only able to patch it up with the help of the wheelwright. His wagon was a little bigger than most but not as big as Old Tine Elliot's. Funny, I hadn't thought about him for a while, but now I considered he was better off not coming on this trip. For surely his big wagon, which he was so proud of, would be destroyed. Before they had a chance to destroy my wagon, another easier route was found that followed Wills Creek north and away from Sandy Gap.

There was no end to the hurdles of nature in our path. Big Savage Mountain lived up to its name. There were stones and boulders everywhere, some bigger than a house and requiring the skills of the miners to blow them into manageable rubble. It was dangerous and backbreaking work. In about a week, we reached a place called Little Meadow that had good forage for the horses. Despite my efforts to find food for them, they had lost weight, and they enjoyed being able to graze again. We rested here a few days.

Being with the advance group afforded me the opportunity to witness the trials and tribulations of building a military road through the wilderness. I was so grateful that, to this point, neither I or my horses were pressed into laboring on the road. Building a twelve-foot-wide road through a wilderness of rocky mountain ridges, thick underbrush, huge virgin forests, and water (trickles, springs, creeks, streams, rivers, and swamps), was a daunting, formidable task.

Trees were cut off low to the ground so wagon axles could pass over the stumps. To do this, there were sawyers or "hatchet men" wearing leather aprons to saw and hack through the old growth timber. The problem with not removing the stumps was when it rained—and it did rain hard—the wagons would sink in the mud and hang up on the stumps.

The timbers were used to build bridges and to make "corduroy" roads through the marshes. This process consisted of laying logs side by side creating a wooden road to ride over the swamp. This kept the wagons from sinking in the muck; but the jarring was hard on the wagons, horses, and men. Because it was an uneven surface, the footing for horses and drivers was difficult, and the constant violent vibrations rattled the wagons with teeth-chattering force.

Rather than going straight up an incline, the engineers used a switchback design, which meant digging out the side of a mountain. Dirt was taken from the upside of a hill and dumped on the down-side to create a roadbed. The more gradual the ascent/descent meant that there was a series of curves as the road zigzagged its way on its course up/down the mountain. Experienced miners, said to be from the lead mines of Bristol, England, used their skills to blast their way through boulders and rocks with gunpowder.

I overheard Col. Washington comment, "Instead of pushing on with vigor without regarding a little rough road, they were halting to level every Mold Hill, and to erect bridges over every brook. By what means, we were four days getting twelve miles."

The more I witnessed of this great endeavor, I had to grudgingly give General Saint Clair credit for the foresight and planning it took to bring this all together. Who would have thought to bring sailors' and miners' skills to the frontier? Logistics was beginning to have real meaning to me.

19

"The very face of the country is enough to Strike
a Damp in the most resolute mind."
—Unknown British Officer

To me, the forests were a beautiful and wonderful place, full of life; but to the army, it was the enemy, seeming dead set on stopping their intrusion into its wilderness. To them, the tree branches and scrubs were like tentacles reaching out to grab them and pull them into the surrounding black gloom. All the soldiers' nerves were on edge. There was a feeling of foreboding as they faced the intimidating forests with trees so tall, they blocked out all sunlight.

One such place was called the Shades of Death as white pines and hemlocks soared hundreds of feet into the sky. Where there were fewer trees, there was brush so thick that you couldn't see three feet into it and swamps so mucky that your boots would be sucked off as you attempted to walk through it. The soldiers guarding our flanks rarely went more than a few yards beyond our road because of the rough terrain. Perhaps they also stayed close because of their desperate fear of an Indian attack.

Even worse than the debilitating gloom and doom among the men was the physical hardships they faced. The hard and dangerous work of felling trees, swinging axes, being a sawyer, and blasting and removing rocks, took its toll. Men suffered hernias, slipped discs, torn and bruised muscles, and extreme fatigue. Felling trees and tree limbs, along with wounds from errant axes, cutting and gashing human limbs, resulted in hideous wounds—and even death. Bites from rattlesnakes and copperhead snakes added to the suffering.

Laborers were soon covered with scratches from plants like, thorn apple and greenbrier vine. Some of the worst agony came from some of the smallest critters—mosquitoes or skeeters, ticks, and chiggers. Bodies covered with welts, the men were driven to distraction with itching. Unfamiliar with poison ivy, they not only suffered from handling it; but in their ignorance, they also burned it among other brush to stand in the smoke to repel insects.

Any exposed parts of the body were soon covered with itching welts. They were truly as pathetic and miserable a group of human beings as I had ever seen. Fortunately, the Indians allies and some of the colonial troops warned of the poison ivy and provided a concoction of wild mint and bear grease to repel the insects. I believe the mint was an attempt to disguise the disgusting bear smell.

There was another problem harder to deal with—malnutrition. Their ration consisted of salted meat and moldy bread laced with sand and dirt and baked in ground ovens. They often drank tainted water; with their fatigue and great thirst, they couldn't always take time to find clean water. This resulted in the "bloody flux" or dysentery, which caused severe diarrhea, cramping, and dehydration. Again, the few Indian allies we had helped by bringing in freshly killed deer and turkey, but their real job was scouting and not food gathering. I may have suffered the same fate, except for the company I kept; Daniel and John were both natural hunters and knew how to survive under adverse conditions.

One morning, while we were camped at Fort Cumberland, Daniel came into camp carrying a gutted and skinned carcass.

"What is—was that?"

I thought it might be a "whistle pig" or groundhog, which we consumed back home. The flesh was generally dark but tender and sweet; after all, their diet was grass.

"It's a raccoon," he replied, "caught it in a snare trap last night."

As we cooked it over an open fire, the grease sizzled, releasing an aroma that made my mouth water.

"Not bad. A little tough, but it has a good flavor. Can you show me how to set snares?"

He showed me how to place a drawstring along a worn game trail so the animal would walk headfirst into the string and strangle itself. We continued to trap all the way along our route to Fort Duquesne. We got rabbits and even a turkey to supplement our diet, but I drew the line at opossum. I knew some people ate them as a regular part of their diet; but to me, they looked like big, ugly rats. They consumed anything dead or alive—mice, rats, birds, whatever was available. To me they were unclean. When I refused to eat it, John chided me, "You ain't a man till you ate good stringy opossum meat!" Another meat I hesitated to eat at first was rattlesnake, but once I gave it a try, I found it was surprisingly tasty.

I always had a natural attraction to water of any kind; and as we traveled, we passed or crossed over springs, trickles, creeks, streams, and rivers. Ma had also taught me about plants and herbs, so I put my knowledge to work. One day, I came into camp with a bucket of greens.

An inquisitive Daniel asked, "What you got there?"

I replied, "Dinner! It's watercress!"

"I ain't no rabbit!" said John.

"We eat it at home. Ma says it is super nutritious, and I know for a fact it has a pleasing mustard-like flavor."

They both ate some and John said, "This is a great addition to our meals."

I started to speak, "I am mor—"

Daniel cut me off and said, "We know. You are more than just another pretty face!"

We all laughed.

In the swamp areas, there were cattails everywhere. I harvested young leaves to eat and pulled out the roots, which when cleaned, we cooked like a potato. "A little rabbit meat, some wild onion, cattail roots, and watercress over an open fire, and you have the tastiest rabbit stew you could ever want."

When I was a young boy, I would catch crayfish and frogs, mostly for fun; but now it was another contribution to our food supply. I would carefully wade in a stream's shallow waters and quietly lift a rock. When the current quickly cleared any cloudy sediment away, if I saw a crayfish, I would plunge my hand into the water and snatch up the little morsel. I knew they always swim backward, so I adjusted my aim accordingly. Granted, it took a lot of crawdads to make a meal for four men, but it was worth it because they were very tasty. We threw them into a pot of boiling water, and when they turned red, we would shell and eat the meaty tail.

I would also search the shallows for frogs. Some of the waters had bullfrogs as big as Dan Morgan's fist. When I brought some frogs back to camp, John exclaimed "You don't expect me to eat those Frenchies do you?" We all had a good laugh and ate heartily. As we were eating, John started making noises, "*Rrrrp, rrrrp... Ribbet, ribbet... Burup, burup...* Now look what ya done! You've gone and made a Frenchie out of me!"

We also took pains to drink clean water, searching out isolated springs and boiling water and making sassafras tea from the bark of the tree roots with the same name.

It was a good time in my life despite the many hardships on the road. I can't remember a time when I laughed so much. I had always been a hard worker, but now it felt good to also be a contributing member of our little group. I always wanted to be considered a man or pretended to be one, but now I felt I belonged. I really felt like a man.

20

"Under a rocky hill where 150 or 200 hundred French and
Indians had encamped ye night before. They had drawn many
odd figures on ye trees expressing with red paint, ye scalps and
Prisoners they had taken with them; there were three french
Names wrote there, Rochefort, Chauraudray and Picauday."
—Unknown British Officer

June 1755

Horses suffered even more than the men on this march. Uneven terrain, often muddy and slippery from hard rains, resulted in fractured
legs. They were attacked by the same insects that plagued the men,
as well as flies that seemed to delight in hanging on faces, particularly on their eyes. Snakes were another shared danger. Due to lack
of good forage at many places along the road and the heavy work
required of them, most were malnourished. In their desperate hun-
ger, they would eat whatever was available, including mountain lau-
rel, which was poisonous. As the trek progressed, the horses became
so weak that soldiers were pressed into service, pushing and pulling
the wagons with them.

I made an extra effort to secure forage for Black, Brown, Dusty,
and Saddle. I had promised Pa I would take good care of them. Their
workload and limited food did result in some weight loss, but they
were in relatively good shape considering the circumstances. Armed
with a sickle, I often went far afield to gather grass and edible plants
for them. I also shared our watercress with them.

I was no fool and was fully aware of the dangers of hostiles lurk-
ing about. I was careful to practice the survival tactics taught to me

by Daniel and John (the same John captured by the Indians because they "smelled" him). I attempted to walk silently, careful not to snap any twigs or rustle any leaves. I paused often to listen for unnatural sounds, like songbirds going silent or crows cawing a warning. I chuckled to myself, trying to figure out how not to stink!

One day, while gathering watercress, I became careless and daydreamed about Sarah. I never heard him approach; I just felt a presence and looked up, and there he stood—an Indian warrior. He was shirtless, and his muscular torso was accentuated with a shiny coating of bear grease. He had an ornament around his neck made of bear claws. He wore a loincloth to cover his manhood and leather leggings to protect his legs. On his feet, he wore leather moccasins fastened at the top with deer strings. There was ornamental beadwork on the leggings and moccasins. His hair was shiny black and braided.

He held a musket in one arm and had a tomahawk and knife stuffed in his belt. He exuded strength and by his undetected approach, cunning. I looked at my musket, but his eyes told me, "Don't even think about it!" I thought I was about to meet my Maker. I prayed in my mind, "Lord Jesus, have mercy on me." By now sweat was dripping off my brow profusely, but instead of attacking me, he spoke in a calm voice in *English*.

"I am Chief Monocatootha of the Oneida nation. I scout for the English, and I have seen you at the wagons. What is your name?"

"J—Jost…Jost Herbach," I stammered.

"Well, Jost, all that yellow hair on your head would make a fine trophy. If you want to keep your hair, you'll need to be more careful."

My hand immediately shifted to my head as if to make sure my scalp was still there. He smiled as he saw the relief on my face, and now, I could see the noble bearing in his.

"You are fortunate no French and their Indian allies are in this area now. What are you doing playing with plants in the water?"

"I am foraging for food for my companions and for my horses. Camp provisions are low and barely edible."

"My son and I are hunting to provide meat for the army. It is sad to see men and horses in such a pathetic state. You are a clever boy"—even then I flinched a little at being called a boy—"and your willingness to take care of your friends and horses is a good thing. But again I would warn you to be on guard at all times."

I nodded in agreement. Then he said something somewhat shocking to me.

"You look like you could be a little brother to Conotocaruis."

"Who is that?"

"Conotocaruis is your Colonel Washington. He was given the name by his friend, Chief Half-King. His great grandfather, John Washington, was originally given the name because he destroyed a Susquehannock village. It means 'village destroyer.'"

I was perplexed. "Why call the colonel a village destroyer when it was his relative that did it?"

"Half-King said he saw a future where young Washington would follow in his ancestors' footsteps. For this reason, he is held in fearful regard by my people."

He sat and shared some pemmican with me as we spoke about food, the army, and the French. Before he departed, he said, "I will give you an Oneida name. *I-laks ohne kanus laht tyelise*, which means 'eats water leaf.'"

We grasped hands and arms, and in an instant, he disappeared into the wilderness. As I *carefully* returned to our camp, I considered how fortunate I was. There are hundreds of hostiles in the area and less than a dozen friendly Indian allies. Thank God I encountered the right Indian!

Daniel, John, and Old Dan were shocked when I told them my slightly embellished story.

"You're damn lucky it was a friendly savage or…well, you would look like me!" exclaimed John as he rubbed his bald dome.

"Twern't luck at all! God was lookin' out for you this day." Daniel chimed in.

Old Dan, with a look of bewilderment on his face, said, "If you ain't somethin'! First, you dine with Ben Franklin, then you got Colonel Washington saluting you, and now you meet an Oneida chief that befriends you with an Indian name! What was that name again?"

"I don't know for sure. It sounds like 'ilack old kanes light trellis.'"

"I know some Oneida talk from trading with them, and it sure enough means 'eats water leaf.' At least he didn't call you *ohrn; kanus lukwe.*"

"What does that mean?"

"Water boy!" They all laughed good-naturedly at my expense.

Old Dan in his gruff manner exclaimed, "Next thing you know, General Braddock himself will be adopting you as his son!"

"No thanks! I've got a Pa, and he is a good one." As an afterthought, I added, "After all, he fathered me, didn't he?"

There were smiles and guffaws all around. *Yes, sir*, I thought, *I was definitely becoming a good wagoner.*

Only a few days later, events happened that made my encounter with the chief even more meaningful. First, word came through the ranks that Chief Monocatootha and his son had been captured by the French and some seventy warriors. The French wanted to kill them, but the Indians respected Monocatootha, so he and his son were tied to a tree and later escaped. The qualities of strength and leadership I saw in him was obviously not lost on his fellow Indians.

We were always crossing some body of water; sometimes it was the same creek or river several times. On June 24, we crossed the Youghiogheny River. It was about a hundred yards wide and three feet deep with a very strong current. Rather than being viewed as an obstacle, the men saw it as a relief from the constant thickets they had been marching through, and it was also a respite from the intense heat of the day.

I mention this crossing because on the other side of the river, we came upon a small stockade. This log fort had been built last year by Indian women to secure themselves and their children against Colonel Washington when he was in the area engaging the French. We named it the Squaw Fort. Though I did not understand why the colonel was given his grandfather's name, there was no doubt the Indians took it seriously.

Hostile sightings and attacks increased, and at a place called the Scalping Camp, a fellow wagoner was attacked. At 4:00 AM, he went to fetch his horses when he was shot in the stomach. Somehow, he made it back to camp. It took him two painful days to die. Four more wagoners were killed and scalped before the savages were driven off. The number of incidences like this increased, and a sense of gloom enveloped us. I did not personally witness these events, but news of attacks spread quickly through the ranks.

As I reflected on all of this, I considered how fortunate I had been. We often think bad things happen to others but never happen to us. I realized how close I had come to being a victim, but I had learned my lesson and limited future excursions beyond the camp.

Later, we approached a recently used hostile camp (the fires were still burning). There we saw bragging and taunts written in red on the trees, including some by the French. They referred to us as "sheep shaggers" and *andouille Anes* (dumbasses) and *ne pas avoir de boules* (let's just say cowards). Rather than intimidating the men, these insults fueled their anger and desire for revenge.

21

"My illness was too violent to suffer me to ride; therefore, I was indebted to a covered wagon for some part of my transportation; but even in this, I could not continue far, for the jolting was so great, that I was left upon the road with a guard and necessities, to wait the arrival of the Dunbar detachment, which was two days march behind us, the General giving his word of honor, that I should be brought up before he reached the French Fort."
—George Washington June 28, 1755

"The 8th of July I rejoined (in a covered wagon) the advance division of the army under the immediate Command of the General [Braddock]."
—George Washington

It dawned on me it that had been several days since I had seen Colonel Washington. I hadn't seen much of Tim either since he was in the vanguard of the army and I was bringing up the rear. It was a happy time when Tim was able to visit with us for a while. He was the purveyor of all army news (gossip), including how he had briefly seen Washington enter and leave Braddock's command tent and that he looked poorly. I didn't think too much about this and went on to enjoy Tim's always merry company.

The next day, I was tending the horses, rubbing liniment on Black's legs when a soldier approached.

"Are you Jost Herbach?"

"I am."

"Come with me. Colonel Washington wishes to see you." I was perplexed but did as I was ordered.

When I entered the colonel's tent, I was staggered by what I saw and smelled. My hand immediately went to cover my nose. The environs wreaked of excreta—it was a sick smell, even worse than a latrine. It was unbearably hot, yet there lay the colonel shivering in a pool of sweat. He had a gaunt appearance. Not a heavy man to begin with, he had lost weight and suffered from fever and chills. His skin was pale, and his lips parched. He obviously suffered from severe cramps as he lay on his side in an almost fetal position. Most striking were his eyes; the confident, almost arrogant look was gone and replaced by a dull listlessness totally out of character for this man.

In my stunned state, I stood there in silence until I finally mumbled, "Wagoner Jost Herbach reporting, sir."

To my utter amazement, he stirred to look at me. In a weak voice, he said, "Don't be so shocked. I have suffered illnesses worse than this. Black canker, river fever, and smallpox, to name a few. I will weather this 'bloody flux' as well!"

I wasn't sure if he was delirious or serious. Actually, he was both, but definitely more of the latter. He continued, "As you can see, I am in no shape to ride a mount, so I am requesting you to take me forward in your covered wagon." Of course, I readily agreed. Most of the contents of my wagon were shifted to other wagons, and leaves were placed as bedding for my passenger.

I already described how primitive the road was, and I could hear moans and groans from the colonel with every bump. His joints must have already ached from his fever, and now each bump in the road added to his misery by bruising and scraping all parts of his body in contact with the hard wagon bed. His dysentery wreaked havoc on his bowels, and he developed an extremely painful rectal abscess.

I soon found myself helping to care for him in the most unpleasant of situations. During breaks in travel and at night, I would give him sips of water and place a wet compress on his forehead. His prescribed diet was diluted barley water, flaxseed tea, and a watery gruel. I determined that this diet would make a healthy man ill! I did vary his diet slightly with pine needle tea and sassafras tea.

I thought about what else I could do to help him. Ma often made a blackberry tea to soothe diarrhea; and wouldn't you know, after miles of struggling through briers and brambles, now there were no blackberry plants to be seen! She also used poultices—which was a mass of material made of mustard, onion, or even cow manure—placed on the hurting part of the body to draw out the poison. Ma once used a mustard poultice on my chest when I had lung congestion. It worked!

Thank God I was never treated with a cow manure poultice! I had none of the materials needed for this remedy, except manure; and I wasn't sure horse turds could be substituted for cow plops. I had a feeling of helplessness being unable to ease the suffering of my companion.

Someone else took an interest in Washington's health. It was General Braddock himself. He came to see the colonel and was as shocked, as I had been, by his appearance. I could see genuine concern on his face. He ordered me to leave my charge at the Bear Camp with a guard. He would stay there, unable to move, until Colonel Dunbar's army reached him.

He gave his word of honor to a distraught Washington that he would bring him forward as they approached Fort Duquesne. He recognized how badly he wanted to participate in the upcoming battle. The general also had his personal physician provide Doctor James Powder, a patented medicine, to ease his discomfort. Later, Washington said it provided immediate relief, but I think his spirit lifted just knowing the general took an interest in his well-being.

At times, the army was stretched out over five miles and was moving at a snail's pace. At the Little Meadows Camp, General Braddock made a decision to divide his army into two groups: the flying column and the supply column. The flying column was to consist of 1,200 of his best men—chosen mainly from his Irish veterans of the 48th and 44th regiments—that would move forward quickly, unencumbered by artillery and wagons.

He sifted out most of the American recruits and assigned them to the supply column. Only a few artillery pieces and a limited number of supply wagons, including mine, accompanied the advance group. A wagon loaded with Indian presents to bargain with the native population was part of this first group. I would learn later how important this was.

The supply column, under the command of Colonel Dunbar, would follow at a slower pace with heavier wagons, baggage, and the heavier artillery. Dunbar was encumbered by a lack of horses. The better horses and wagons accompanied General Braddock. Dunbar could only advance a few miles then send the horses he had back to bring the rest of the army forward. This was a tedious and time-con- suming task. Since my wagon carried only a small cargo and Colonel Washington, Dusty and Saddle were commandeered to be used as packhorses. Black and Brown, despite having lost some weight, were capable of pulling the wagon with its reduced load. I would never see my brothers' horses again.

After leaving Washington at the Bear Camp, I continued along with the flying column. When we were approaching the Monongahela River, twelve miles or so from our target, an orderly came to me with orders to return to the main army and fetch Colonel Washington. Upon my return, he gave me a weak smile as I drove up to him. I saluted, and he was able to return it.

He still looked washed out—pale, thin, and still feverish—but he was lucid and was able to walk, although tenderly, to the wagon. *How*, I wondered, *would this man be able to fight in a battle?* We hitched his mount to the wagon and pressed on to the lead army. Upon arriving, he took the pillow he carried with him and his mount and reported to headquarters. He thanked me for my assistance. He was not profuse, but I knew he was sincere in his gratitude.

22

"As to my body, where the leaf falls, let it rot."
—Captain Robert Cholmely, 48ᵗʰ Regiment

"The plight of the wounded, jolted along the uneven road in wagons, as maggots grew in their wounds, can only be imagined."
—George Washington

"The dead—the dying—the groans-lamentations-
and crys along the road of wounded for help…
were enough to pierce a heart of adamant."
—George Washington

July 9–12, 1755

What am I doing here? Will I survive? Will any British survive? Dear God help me! What should I do?

I was contemplating following the example of Daniel Boone and cutting a horse loose from the reins and fleeing when out of the chaos, I heard a familiar voice. "No."

It wasn't God. It was Colonel Washington.

"Jost, get those two officers out of that abandoned wagon next to you, and place them in yours. Put any other wounded you can get in with them, and then get out of here! Get back across the river quickly." He had seen my bloody face and asked, "Are you hurt bad?"

With my hand reaching up to my forehead, I replied, "No, it's just a scratch."

I transferred Captain Roger Morris, who had an ugly wound to his nose, making it hard for him to breathe, and Captain Robert

Orme, who was wounded in the leg, to my wagon. As I was getting them into my wagon, a British soldier was helping a wounded man to the relative safety of the wagons. As we added this wounded man to my "wounded wagon," his companion said, "Zebulon was shot by a savage who was starting to scalp him alive. I shot the bloody hostile before he could finish the job. Take good care of him."

The brave soldier returned to Washington's small defensive perimeter. I never saw him again. Upon quick inspection, I saw his friend had an awful leg wound but the more horrible wound was on his scalp. It had been half cut off on one side; and on that side, he was bloody, and his face was sagging. His scalp was like a flap that could be lifted to expose his skull. I would have thrown up, but there was nothing left in my retching stomach. I did not see how he was alive or would continue to live. I crammed three more wounded men into the wagon, unhobbled the horses, and made tracks for the river.

Shots followed us into the river, and I heard bullets thud into the tailgate and whiz around me and the horses; but we came out onto the bank unscathed. Without any urging from me, the team raced back over the same road we had just traversed with such hardship. We were accompanied by two other wagons and by the tumbril (a two-wheeled cart) carrying the badly wounded General Braddock. He had been shot with a bullet passing through his right arm and puncturing his lung. He was in obvious pain and in a feeble state but was still giving orders.

Washington himself, sick and exhausted, announced he had been ordered to ride ahead to inform Colonel Dunbar of the day's awful proceedings and to get help. The rest of us feared the Indians would be pursuing us, so we pressed on as rapidly as possible. We kept moving well into the night. The night was filled with pitiful moans and groans not only from poor passengers but also from the wounded and dying along the road. We finally stopped when the horses were too exhausted to continue. Despite being bone-weary, no one slept because we feared an imminent attack by bloodthirsty savages. We pushed the horses and soon returned to our forlorn journey.

At daybreak, we stopped again to rest the animals. I took this time to assess the wounded, the wagon, the horses, and myself. I had no training or experience to deal with what I saw as I tried to attend to the suffering men. During the night, one of my charges had died. I said a prayer over his body as we placed it along the side of the road. We had no digging tools, time, or energy to bury him. As I inspected the wounds, I felt overwhelmed and useless. Jagged pieces of lead and flattened slugs were still in some wounds. *Should I remove them? Will they bleed to death?* Even if I tried to help, I had no tools; in fact, I didn't have anything to even clean the wounds.

I ripped the dead man's tattered shirt into strips to cover the wounds. It was all I could do. Within a day or so, maggots infested the injuries. I did take the time to cut some pine boughs to line the wagon bed for their comfort and gave them a drink of water at every stop. One poor man died as I tended him. He tried to speak but was so feeble that I only caught two words: *pray* and *Katie*. I saw relief on his face as I prayed for him. As for Katie, I suppose he was trying to tell me to inform his loved one of his death and love. Sadly, I never knew his name.

An inspection of the wagon shocked me. There were dozens of bullet holes in the splintered sideboards and tattered tailgate, but more appalling were the conditions of the wheels—all the tiers were loose, and the axles were worn and loose. I used my hammer pin and pounded pieces of hardwood into the slack fittings. This was a poor and temporary repair at best.

The horses were exhausted. Black had a gash on his right side that must have been a "near miss" bullet wound. Despite everything, their legs were all sound, and the extraordinary measures I had taken to provide forage for them earlier was paying off now. I reflected on how proud I was of Black and Brown, who, though terrified, responded to my voice and the reins and did not bolt. Pa always says, "Good stock equals good results!" Seems Pa had a saying for every situation.

Finally, I took stock of myself. I was filthy, my hat was long gone, and my hair felt long and shaggy—but I was glad it was still there. I was covered in blood, some mine but most from handling the dead and wounded. Both my shirt and breeches were ripped and torn, and I discovered an ugly gash on my arm. I had no idea where it had come from; maybe it was a near miss from during the battle. I was hungry and bone-weary, but I was alive with no serious wounds.

I questioned why God would allow this kind of horror to happen, but I remembered the preacher back home saying God gave us free will—so really, *we* allowed it to happen. Ma always says faith is easy when things are going well, but it is when we are faced with adversity that real faith shines through. I thanked God for his provision for me and asked for his help to fulfill my mission to get these men to a safe place and help.

We reached Dunbar's army (a distance of sixty miles) in three days. What we found was a scene of chaos.

23

"Scandalous as the action [battle] was, more scandalous
was the based and hurried retreat, with the immense
destruction and expenses to the nation."
—Unidentified British Officer

General Braddock died much lamented by the whole army.
—Royal Naval Officer

July 11–18, 1755

When we arrived at Dunbar's Camp, we were met with despair and
panic. We learned that on the previous day, terrified wagoners—
including my fellow Pennsylvanians, Matt Laird and Mike and Jake
Hoover—spread the news of the defeat in the most horrific detail.
They said most of the army were killed, including General Braddock
and officers Sir Peter Halket and Captain Orme.

Later that day, George Washington arrived in camp providing a
more accurate account of events (which, of course, were still *horrible*).
Dunbar ordered his men to arms to establish a defensive perimeter.
Everyone expected the Indians to pursue and attack. The troops were
also there to prevent desertion. Having spread fear and trepidation
among the army, Laird and the Hoovers sneaked out of camp and
went on to spread the same dread to Fort Cumberland and beyond.

Upon our arrival, the surviving wounded were finally given
proper medical attention. Amazingly, both Morris and Orme survived their injuries. The last I heard, the scalped man Zebulon also
survived and became a local hero, telling quite dramatically how "I

cheated the Indians from getting my hair!" Sadly, many others were not so fortunate.

After seeing that my wounded charges were taken care of, I tended the horses, feeding and grooming them; and then, completely exhausted, I curled up into a ball and slept deeply despite all the turmoil around me. I awoke to huge bonfires burning everything that could not be taken with us. General Braddock ordered a retreat; and since there were only enough horses and wagons left to transport the wounded, everything—artillery, ammunition, tents, all excess baggage, even damaged wagons—were destroyed so they would be of no use to the enemy.

When Indians approached the defensive perimeter, the sentries deserted their posts and ran as if they were seeing the devil himself. Fortunately, the Indians were Braddock's scouts and posed no threat. They did bring good news: the Indians were *not* coming. In a bloodlust, the French Indians were gathering trophies from the dead and wounded, including scalps, firearms, and clothing. They said the battlefield was littered with stripped and mutilated bodies, including those of Braddock's seven women companions.

The real prize that hindered any pursuit was the hostiles' discovery of the wagon with "Indian trade goods" and a couple of hogsheads of ale. It was the general's plan to use the goods to pacify the Indians after their defeat. They served better now by keeping the hostiles from further attacks. According to the scouts, the French and Indians never crossed the Monongahela River. Though this was good news, it did little to dispel the anxiety that had taken root in the hearts and minds of the army.

On July 13, we exited Dunbar's Camp, leaving behind only pillars of smoke from the funeral pyres of men and supplies. Later that same day, General Braddock finally expired, ending his suffering and pain. Services were held over his burial plot in the middle of the road. The retreating army then marched over the site so the heathens could not find and excavate his body for desecration. Braddock's defeat had now become Dunbar's retreat.

On July 15, Colonel Washington was ordered to take the lightly wounded ahead to Fort Cumberland escorted by seventy men. I was part of that convoy. Hysteria reigned at the fort. Anguished wives ran to us looking for their husbands or kin. They pleaded for information about their loved ones. Their soulful weeping and wailing touched my heart and made me feel awful.

A woman sobbing hysterically ran from wagon to wagon, calling, "John! John Hood!" She questioned anyone who would listen, "Do you know my John? Do you know where he is?"

I felt her anguish, but all I could do was offer false hope.

"There are stragglers following us on foot. He may come in over the next day or two."

She gripped my hand and then moved on to the next wagon. There were a few cries of joy as some families were reunited, but for most, it was no news or sad news. It got me to thinking how those wagoners were spreading doom and gloom before them. *If they continue to tell the same stories all the way back home, what would my family think? They would probably think I was killed. When I get back, would they be in mourning, or would they be holding out hope that I could still return?*

We were only in the fort a short time until I received an unexpected visit from George Washington. He looked awful; and again I wondered how he could still walk, considering his illness and all he had been through. What really surprised me was he sought me out to give me advice and aid.

"Jost, take your horses, your musket, and any supplies you can muster. Your wagon has served well, but it is beyond salvaging. Leave it and go home!" When I started to protest, he interrupted, "You have fulfilled your obligations here. The battle has been lost. Colonel Dunbar has ordered a full retreat to winter quarters in Philadelphia. Here, take this." He handed me a fine shirt. "Yours is bloody and tattered beyond repair."

I was stunned. He had taken the time and consideration to help me in these chaotic times. I thanked him and he continued, "Take the Fredrick Road east along the Potomac River. There will be less chance of a hostile raid. Team up with one of the frontier families heading east. They are leaving because there will be no protection against Indian raids once the army moves out. You'll be safer in their company, and at the same time, you can help them on the journey."

I actually began to tear up when he gave me a weak salute and said, "Providence continue to be with you!"

I responded in kind and said, "God bless you!"

Then he was gone.

24

"Love is the most beautiful of dreams and the worst of nightmares."
—Aman Jassal

"Hieeeeeeeyah!" The Indian war cries shrieked in my ears, went to my brain, went down, and settled in my heart, instilling what it was meant to—fear. We had been fighting off a hostile attack, but the tide seemed to be turning against us. The children were crying as I hid them in the cold cellar under the house. I could hardly breathe, and my eyes stung in the smoke-filled room. My wife, Sarah, heavy with our third child, was fighting with the spirit of a she bear protecting her cubs.

We had kept a fire going in the hearth to keep them from coming down the chimney flue. We heard them on the roof; they were covering the chimney, causing the smoke to go back into the cabin. We were forced to put out the fire so we could breathe. While we were firing our muskets, including the one issued to me in Carlisle in May of 1755, through the small gun portals in the wall, hostiles came down the chimney. I turned to face a savage and fell backward onto the floor with him on top of me. He had a tomahawk in one hand and a knife in the other; and I was using all my strength, holding his wrists to keep him from plunging either weapon into my body.

Then I heard her say, "Jost…Jost…Help! Jost, help me!"

In terror, I turned my head to see a familiar hostile, painted half red and half black. He was savagely holding Sarah by her long hair and was wielding a knife over her heart.

"No, no, no… God, please *no*!" I sobbed.

The cry continued, "Jost! Jost!"

"Jost! Jost! Wake up! It's a bad dream."

Straddling me was Jedidiah Kramer. He was holding my thrashing arms to protect himself. I looked again, and Sarah was gone. It was indeed a horrible dream, one I had been having since the Battle of the Monongahela River. The Indian in the dream was familiar because he was the same one that had slaughtered young Tim Murphy before my eyes. I was drenched in sweat.

As I gathered my wits, I apologized to Jed, who was very understanding. This had not been the first nightmare I had, had since the massacre. It concerned me not only because it interrupted my sleep and my companion's sleep, but also because in our community, dreams were believed to have importance and meaning. *What did this dream mean? Would I lose Sarah as I had lost my friend Tim?* It bothered me that I did not have the ability to interpret dreams like some of the folks back home.

I readily accepted Washington's advice; and after our parting, I saw a tired, bedraggled family pulling a tumbril with all their worldly possessions in it. They were all struggling to keep the cart moving. I approached and introduced myself. I proposed that we travel together to help one another and for safety reasons. They saw my musket and the two horses and immediately realized the benefit of working together. I suggested one horse could pull the cart while the other one rested, or the missus and children could take turns riding the spare horse. We shook hands, and introductions were made all around.

The father was Jedidiah Kramer. He was a tall man, lean but strong-looking. He had a dark complexion and intelligent eyes. I noticed he was missing a pinky finger on his left hand. Like everyone else in those times, he looked exhausted and somewhat defeated; after all, his dreams had been shattered. His wife, Deborah (he called her Debbie), had the features of a pretty woman; but the trials and tribulations of subsistence farming and recent events had left her with deep age lines on her face. She was pale and just plain worn out. She carried their youngest child (less than a year old), Isaiah, in a papoose, which meant she was carrying a lot of extra weight.

The first son, Adam, was nine years old. He was thin yet somehow seemed to maintain his youthful vitality and inquisitiveness. Eva was the oldest sibling, twelve going on thirteen, as she was quick to point out. She had reddish-brown hair, hazel eyes, and freckles on her nose. She showed no signs of womanly development, but she was cute. She was rather assertive and outspoken for a girl; but I soon learned she was a responsible and hardworking person, not unlike how I perceived myself. The last introductions were Black and Brown. Adam and Eva loved the horses, and the feeling was mutual. I could almost see the horses smiling with the attention they were receiving. Jed and Deborah loved the horses too, but it was mainly because they wouldn't have to pull the cart themselves.

They described their homestead as a fertile valley, located only ten miles from Great Meadow, where Washington had been defeated at Fort Necessity. They had, had some Indian problems; but it was limited to livestock theft. They had their only horse, a cow, and two pigs stolen; but they themselves were not harmed. They thought the raids would stop after Braddock's victory. With the news of the defeat, they packed up and headed back east, along with almost all the settlers on the frontier.

Washington was right; having traveling companions made the return trip home so much better. There was not a lot of game available to hunt near the road due to the recent heavy traffic; but using the hunting skills and snares I learned from Daniel, we ate fairly well. At least, no one was losing any more weight. When we rested or camped for the night, we would pass the time telling stories.

I asked Jed how he lost his little finger.

"Ya know, it's the things you do best and take for granted that can get you into trouble. You lose your caution and become careless. I was butchering a deer—I've done this hundreds of times—when the blade slipped and cut off the finger. Problem was it was bitter cold, and both hands were about frozen as I worked. It was so cold I couldn't control the knife and so cold I didn't feel the cut at first. There was so much blood you couldn't tell what was mine and what came from the deer. Debbie cleaned and bandaged the little stump. So now, I can only count to nine!"

He laughed at his own joke, and so did I.

Our conversations ranged into many topics—from farming, to food, and even names (yes, names). Jed and Deborah put great stock in giving meaningful names to their children.

"Our firstborn was Eva. Her name comes from the first woman, Eve, which means 'full of life.'"

I couldn't argue with that name, for Eva, for it fit her personality perfectly.

"Of course, Adam was our first son, named after the first man, Adam, from the Book of Genesis. Isaiah is named after the prophet in the Bible. His name means 'to save.'"

I knew both Jedidiah and Deborah were biblical names.

Jed said, "My name means 'friend of God,' and I sure hope I am! Deborah was a female warrior and a savior of her people. Her name means 'bee.' All I can figure is my Debbie is a warrior, and she is always busy as a bee!"

We all chuckled, including Deborah. It was good to laugh again. I reflected on my name Jost. I knew it meant "just," and I hoped I could live up to it. I also thought of how Indian names had meaning, like my Oneida name, "eats water leaf." I liked Jed's dry sense of humor and respected his wisdom and Bible knowledge.

We talked a lot about farming. He was heartsick about abandoning their farm. If he went back, he knew the buildings would be completely destroyed by the savages, and mother nature would be reclaiming the land with weeds and brush. I told him about the limestone outcroppings and fertile land near Raystown. He said that might be a future possibility, but for now, they wanted to recoup and spend time with family back in Philadelphia. Debbie, in particular, had, had enough of frontier hardship. She was a good woman and wife. A kind person, she noted I was living in rags and offered to mend my breeches and my old bloody shirt, which I had saved.

I was a little embarrassed sitting by the fire wrapped in a blanket as she stitched. Adam and Eva had fun at my expense trying to grab my covering from me. I have to admit I enjoyed the friendly bantering. Once mended, I wore my old shirt because I wanted to take good care of my gift from Colonel Washington. It really was a fine shirt. She had Eva clean and tend my head wound and the gash in my arm. It was beginning to feel like I was part of their family, and I liked it.

They were anxious to hear my stories of the "battle." I may have embellished my role and survival "just a wee bit," as Tim would have said. Adam and Eva were greatly impressed, and I must confess I enjoyed being an object of respect. Both children spent as much time with me as they could. They were always asking questions and trying to impress me and get my approval.

The trip was mostly uneventful compared to all that had happened recently, but more than that, it was enjoyable. With each passing mile, we became more relaxed. I knew we were safe when a pair of rufous-sided towhees merrily escorted us along the road. These friendly birds would flit from bush to bush, just a few feet from us, as they guided us through their territory. The red-eyed chirper, as we generally called them, made a friendly *chewink* sound that was pleasant to the ear.

As we approached within a few miles of Kreutz Creek, I wanted to mount a horse and gallop home as quickly as possible; but if I did, the other horse pulling the cart would also run, jeopardizing the cart and its contents. The horses solved the dilemma for me. They knew they were close to home, and they wanted to bolt. When I couldn't restrain Black any longer, I hopped on his back, and he took off rapidly toward home. Brown and the bouncing cart were following close behind. The Kramers were trying to run and pick up items flying from the tumbril but couldn't keep up.

25

"The magic thing about home is that it feels good to leave, and it feels even better to come back"

—Anonymous

August 1755

The farm looked deserted. There was no one to be seen. I assumed Pa and the boys were working in the fields, and Ma was probably in the house. Black didn't stop running until he entered the barn and went into his stall. Horses are always quick to return to the barn after a long workday. To them, it meant rest, food, and grooming—it was their home. I dismounted Black as Brown came to the barn. I unhitched her from the cart, and she happily joined Black. They were whinnying like children playing. The whole time I was yelling, "Ma! Pa! Henry! I'm home!"

As I turned around, I was attacked by that wonderful bundle of fur and drool—Tauser. He almost knocked me off of my feet and covered my face with slobber as he kissed me. With him bouncing and barking all around me, I ran for the house. Ma came out and stopped in her tracks. A huge smile broke out on her face as tears filled her eyes. We ran to each other, and she hugged me like she never wanted to let go. Suddenly, I was gripped in a hug from behind. It was Henry, who was also crying and repeating my name over and over.

Ma kept saying, "Praise God! You're alive! My son is alive!"

By now, I was weeping too. Then I heard the deep voice of Pa. "My boy…Jost…alive… Thank you, Lord!"

He got me in a bear hug I thought would pop my head off.

"When we heard the news about Braddock's total defeat, we thought you were dead. It has been a solemn and gloomy place here these last few weeks as we each experienced our grief over your loss. How did you make it out alive?"

"I have stories to tell you will find hard to believe! I made friends with George Washington and an Indian chief. I saw things I wish I had never seen. I am here because I believe God was with me and protected me. I will give you all the details later."

"You met an Indian, and he didn't kill you?" asked Henry. "Wow!"

I think I will be an even bigger hero to Henry than before I began this saga.

"And George Washington! In person!" exclaimed Pa.

I quickly got my fine shirt from the cart and told them briefly how it was a gift from the colonel. They were in absolute awe. I asked where Jacob was; and they said they expected him home soon from his own farm, west of York, near my two oldest brothers. He had built a barn and was now working on building a house for Dorcas. They were to be married in September.

The Kramers approached, their arms full of items that had fallen from the speeding cart. They had a sheepish look about them, like they didn't want to intrude on our joyful reunion. Pa, Ma, and Henry all looked at me with a "Who are these people?" look on their faces. I made introductions and gave an abbreviated explanation of the loss of their home and our travel together. Ma embraced them all, and Pa and Jed shook hands.

Always warm and hospitable, Ma invited everyone to supper. We had Sallie Pudding and *schmack-worchts* followed by delicious ginger cake. What a wonderful, congenial time we had! I noticed Henry seemed smitten with Eva, but she kept looking at me. Stories were shared with "ooohs" and "aahs" added at the appropriate times. I did most of the talking and enjoyed being the center of attention.

While all of this was going on, Jacob arrived. When he saw me, he was as shocked as everyone had been. I left the table and greeted him with a warm hug, which he returned. If you'll recall, we had not parted on the best of terms. He readily joined in the festivities and storytelling. I think he was jealous because my presence was taking away from the excitement of his upcoming wedding. Then he said with a smirk, "Too bad about Sarah." Now he had my and everyone's attention.

"What do you mean? Is she all right?"

"Why, she's fit as a fiddle! But when she heard you was dead, she got herself a new beau right away. Word is they're talkin' marriage."

I couldn't speak. I was crushed. Thoughts of Sarah and I getting married and being together kept me going through the hardship I had faced. How could she forget about me and make a commitment to someone else so quickly? Did she grieve for me at all? All the joy I was feeling left me in an instant. I wanted to smack Jacob in the face; instead, I left the now quiet table and went outside to be alone. I could hear Pa scolding Jacob, but it was too late—I was heartbroken.

I cried as I walked and thought. To me, our love was *real*—it was an adult thing—but to her, it must have been just a childish, passing flirtation. Eva had come out of the house and watched me from the porch. When I returned to the house, I saw her sitting there with a tear running down her cheek. She gave me a weak smile of encouragement as I passed.

The next morning, the Kramers were preparing to leave; they were anxious to be united with their family, who were probably worried and wondering about their fate. Pa hitched Camel up to their cart and sent Henry along to bring back the horse. At age eleven, he was excited for this new responsibility, a day trip to Philadelphia and back. We Herbachs didn't always like responsibility, but we never shirked it either. He knew this was a step toward manhood for him.

There were tears as we hugged. Eva cried, "We will never see you again."

"Of course, you will. We're only a half-day ride apart. You can visit and go to church with us on Sundays. And we can visit you, and you can show us around the big city."

Eva seemed a little relieved, but her face showed doubt it would really happen. Often words like these are spoken and never fulfilled, but in this instance, they were. We gathered together many times over the years and loved each other as family.

I became a local hero, and even Sarah flirted to get back in my good graces. But I was too hurt and too smart to fall that way again. I enjoyed my new status in the community and was sure of one thing: it was *geweldig* to be home!

Epilogue

"For I know the plans I have for you," declared
the Lord, "plans to prosper you and not harm
you, plans to give you hope and a future."
—Jeremiah 29:11

June 1828

While placing these memories to paper, I have tried to keep to the facts and feelings as they occurred then. My desire is for the reader to experience what I did. That was a long time ago, and I may have inadvertently let the present slip into the past; but I believe this to be an honest presentation.

I would now like to tie up a few loose ends. If you wondered if Eva and I ever became an item, we did. We were married in 1764. You may ask, "Why did it take so long [nine years] to wed?" She was twenty-one years old, almost an old maid for that time; and I was twenty-five years old, like Jacob, seeming to be a confirmed bachelor. Initially, I saw Eva as a child and a friend. Over time, she became a beautiful woman and an exceptional person. As I became aware of her beauty, I told myself that I didn't want to jeopardize our friendship. I also didn't want to experience rejection again as I had with Sarah Kauffman. It sounds like a cliché, but we became best friends before we became lovers.

Over the years, she was pursued by many admirers, but she always found an excuse to reject them. She later told me she loved me from the time we first met back at Fort Cumberland. Thank goodness she looked at me through the eyes of love and was patient enough to wait for me! One day, we were good-naturedly jostling around, almost like brother and sister, when the intimate proximity of our faces resulted in a sudden kiss. It was a gentle kiss that went right to my heart. The words came easily out of my mouth. "I love you." She responded, "I have always loved you!" The veil of denial had lifted, and a new and wonderful phase of my life began. It lasted until Eva's death after the birth of Susanna, our eighth child, in 1785.

I never saw Daniel Boone, John Finely, or Chief Monocatooha again; but I did reunite with Ben Franklin, George Washington, and Old Dan Morgan. We all saw action together in the great war for independence, but that is another long story for another day. Speaking of Old Dan, shortly after we abruptly parted company at the Battle of the Monongahela, he assaulted a British officer; after all, he was a notorious brawler and despised the British.

For his punishment, he was sentenced to 500 lashes "laid on heavy on the bare back." Men often died from this cruel punishment. Old Dan not only survived but also enjoyed telling anyone who would listen how he was cheated. "The British only applied 499 lashes!" His toughness and leadership abilities led to his being a very successful general during the war for freedom from the British he hated so much. He also became a devout Christian. He was indeed a man's man, a leader of men!

As I reflect back on my life from my eighty-seven-year-old perch, I see what Ma meant about God having a plan for our lives (Jer. 29:11). I was always hatching my schemes, but the whole time, God was in control. He was opening and closing doors for me. For instance, at the Battle of the Monongahela, my inclination was to flee the scene with Daniel Boone. But when I prayed, "God, help me! What should I do?" George Washington showed up with orders to save the wounded. Prayer answered!

I have seen God's hand guiding and protecting me along life's path. It's often been a rocky road of twists and turns, like Braddock's Road; but with faith, hard work, and God's help, I have more than persevered—I have prospered. These four months of my youth, just recounted, helped me to grow into a man. A man who loves the Lord, loves his family, and loves his country. I am indeed a *blessed* man.

Author's Note

Thank you for taking the time to read my book. When I announced to my family and friends that I was going to write a historical fiction novel, some were shocked. They asked, "Why would you do that?" But what some were really thinking was, *Are you capable of writing a book?* I admit I am grammatically challenged; so you, the readers, will help determine how to answer these questions.

There are many reasons why I decided to write. One reason is time. I am retired and now have the time; there was never enough of it in the past. I always thought our forefathers were prolific writers because they didn't have to deal with all the distractions of modern life. Technology didn't rule their lives, and they didn't have movies and professional sports to devour their time; so they put their time to good, productive use. Today, when you get old, you find you are not as enamored with the same things; and many things, like playing basketball, are beyond your capacity to perform, freeing up time. I now have the time, so I write.

I read my first history book when I was thirteen years old (I am now seventy-seven years old). It was about the Carthaginian General Hannibal. It ignited my interest in ancient history. I next read *Caesar's Commentaries* and then anything I could get my hands on about that time in history. My reading then broadened as my interests broadened. I eventually became a secondary high school teacher, a career I pursued for thirty years. Oddly, I never did teach Ancient or Roman history but taught American history.

Over the years, I have read hundreds of history books and articles, both fiction and nonfiction. As they say, "eating at McDonald's doesn't make you a hamburger"; and likewise, reading books doesn't make you a writer. But I thought maybe I could take the knowledge and experiences I have had and produce something of worth and interest, so I write.

My subject was easy to choose. I had a great grandfather on my mother's side, Henry Lee Fisher, who was a judge and an author/poet. He wrote about the Pennsylvania Dutch society with great affection and wanted to preserve their heritage. With pride, he wrote about his grandfather, Jost Herbach.

Very little is known about Jost; there are even variations of the spelling of his last name. He was born on October 11, 1741, and died on August 16, 1832, a long life in any generation. He was robust well into his eighties, riding a mount or sometimes walking to visit his daughter near Antietam, Maryland; then heading north to visit another daughter in Franklin County, Pennsylvania; then returning to York, Pennsylvania—a round trip of 150 miles. He was the fourth of eight children. All that is known about his involvement in the Battle of the Monongahela was that he was a wagoner and survived. I think him a worthy subject, so I decided to "fill in the blanks," and so I write.

I will tell you a few stories from my past that you may recognize from the book, which influenced my writing. As a small child, I "helped" my Grandpa Fisher weed his garden. He straddled a row of red beet seedlings, pulling out the weeds and throwing them to the side. Wanting to be a "big boy helper," I followed him down the row, pulling out the red beet plants. I know there was punishment involved, but it wasn't too severe (I am still here to tell about it!). I have enjoyed gardening to this very day.

I would often bring wildflower bouquets to my mother. She always made a big fuss. "It's a dandelion. Look how it makes my face glow!" she would say as she held it under her chin, and it did! "That's a buttercup or Queen Anne's lace or tiger lily…" Thus I got an early lesson in plants. Wild mint, mulberries, raspberries, blackberries, and other trees and plants all became childhood treasures.

I grew up in a small middle-class suburb with woods and farm fields nearby. There were always great adventures to be had. We tied ropes to tree branches and swung like Tarzan. We built forts of rocks and brush to fend off Indian attacks. We made shields of cardboard boxes and spears of sticks, donned sheets for a robe, and played Roman soldiers. We used our imaginations. We would pack a lunch of sandwiches, apples, cookies, and potato chips or pretzels, and hike about a mile to a stream. We waded up the stream looking for its origin.

Along the way, we built dams and caught salamanders, minnows, and crayfish until we reached its source at a farm pond. We would return home explorers, with tales to tell our parents. To this day, my grandchildren and great grandchildren and I still build dams and catch critters in my creek. My point is if I could grow up learning about and enjoying the great outdoors, why could that not be true of Jost? After all, nature was his workplace and his playground.

As I sit here writing these notes, a hen turkey with nine or ten chicks is passing through my backyard. Birds of all colors and sizes visit my yard: phoebes, robins, indigo buntings, cardinals, catbirds, pileated, downing and red woodpeckers, bluebirds; and yes, even the American bald eagle puts in an appearance. These are just a few of the birds I have witnessed this May in Pennsylvania. The woodland phlox and bush honeysuckle are in full bloom, putting on a colorful display against the verdant green background.

Last summer, I had five bears outside my kitchen door, a mama bear and her four cubs. I could have opened the door and touched a cub. Obviously, I had enough sense not to do that. I've had deer, bobcat, pine martins, mink, and beaver visit my yard and stream. I live near a bison farm, and yes, I tell people I live "where the deer and the buffalo roam."

I must admit that not all wildlife encounters are copacetic. Bear destroyed my bird feeders and deer browse my garden. This morning, I had four squirrels and a chipmunk feasting on green strawberries (they don't even wait for them to ripen). They will be joined by mice, raccoons, and even turtles as the season progresses. See where I get my interest and appreciation for nature and why so much of it is included in the book?

Some readers may think I ascribe too many adult qualities to a fourteen-year-old colonial boy. Here is why I feel justified in my presentation. Remember, the story is the reminiscence of an eighty-seven-year-old man. Certainly, all he has learned over his lifetime, including enhanced vocabulary, would creep into the storytelling. We all tend to remember what we want to about the past—and even to embellish it.

Today we live in a society that sometimes overprotects and spoils youngsters. Maybe this is why so many thirty- and forty-year-olds still live with their parents. In essence, we expect and require little from children today, so we get little. In much of colonial America, children were contributors from an early age. They acted more like adults because it was required of them. It was not uncommon for fourteen-year olds to be wed. An unmarried twenty-one-year-old woman was almost an "old maid."

As you may have already surmised, the book is about Jost, but a lot about myself is incorporated into his character. Posterity records he was, like Washington, a tall man for his time (six feet and two inches), but nothing more was said about his appearance. The physical description in this book is really me in my prime. Some of his doubts and fears, hopes and dreams, reflect what I recall of my own youth.

Like Jost, I am also the product of a large family, the oldest of eleven children. I learned early in life to be a responsible person with a good old-fashioned Pennsylvania Dutch work ethic. I changed more diapers than a nurse in a pediatric ward! In essence, I am a Pennsylvania Dutchman writing about a Pennsylvania Dutchman. For better or for worse, I am Jost and Jost is me!

One important clarification is necessary here: the story of Jost's sexual encounter with Astor and the Thatch Patch is entirely fictional and *not* based on my personal experience. Some of my Christian friends will not like this scene, but it shows how anyone can commit sin and learn from it. There was indeed a Stuckey's Tavern along the route I have Jost following. I chose the Burd Road to include the tavern but also to take Jost through Raystown (now Bedford, Pennsylvania), which is my current home. The Burd Road was under construction at the time and did not fully connect with the Braddock Road till after the battle. I ignored this fact to suit my story line and character development.

The Braddock Road has long since been overtaken by time and progress; but I traveled to Cumberland, Maryland, and loosely followed the route taken by the British army on its trek north to Fort Duquesne (Pittsburgh, Pennsylvania). There were heavy rains most of that day, and creeks and rivers were high and muddy. It made me more appreciative of how formidable a task it was that they had undertaken. I recorded all I could about the terrain, trees, shrubs, wetlands, birds, and wildlife I saw. I incorporated much of this into the book.

I visited Braddock's Grave and Fort Necessity. I also stopped at the Compass Inn Museum in Laughlintown, Pennsylvania, and Fort Ligonier in Ligonier, Pennsylvania. Both places provided a lot of material about the customs of the time period I was researching. They had Conestoga Wagons and replicas of the type of farm wagon Jost would have used.

One thing that amazed me in my research was the contradictory information available. When in doubt, I chose the information that best suited my story line. Like many historical fiction novels I have read, I have slightly altered some facts and timelines to suit my story; but I believe the book to be fundamentally, historically sound.

I want to thank my daughters, Deborah Piliukaits and Sarah Carletti, for their encouragement and support. I also thank my brother, Jeff Lau, and my sister, Pam Geiselman, for their support and my grandson Eric Schrum for all his technical help. In the accompanying bibliography, I mention just a few of the many sources that informed and inspired me. As a neophyte and aspiring writer, I don't presume to be in their league, but I thank them for the enjoyment and inspiration they provided me.

I have been a widower for six years; but everything I do is still inspired by my wife, Martha. She taught me so much in our fifty-three years together. I love and miss her. I guess I am just a silly old romantic at heart. We both always enjoyed books and movies with happy endings, so I ended on the happy note of Eva and Jost marrying, which is what really happened.

Finally, I describe Jost as a blessed man; and like him, I am also a blessed man—and this too is why I write.

Thank you for reading!

R. Greg Lau

Bibliography

This is only a tiny part of materials used in my research, but these were the most helpful and inspiring sources.

Baker, Norman L. *Braddock Road: Mapping the British Expedition from Alexandria to the Monongahela*. Charleston: The History Press, 2013.

Berkebile, Donald H. *Conestoga Wagons in Braddock's Campaign, 1755*. 2009.

Born, Jason. *The Long Fuse* (5 historical fiction books on the French and Indian War). Great Space, 2017.

Eckert, Allen W. *Wilderness Empire: A Narrative*. Boston: Little Brown and Company, 1969.

Every, Dale Van. *Forth to the Wilderness: The First American Frontier, 1754–1774*. William Morrow and Company, 1964.

Fisher, H. L. *Olden Times: Or, Pennsylvania Rural Life Some Fifty Years Ago, and Other Poems*. York, Pa.: Fisher Bros. Publishers, 1888.

Fisher, H. L. *The Old Market House on the Square*. York, Pa.: The York Republican, 1879.

Preston, David L. *Braddock's Defeat: The Battle of the Monongahela and the Road to Revolution.* Oxford University Press, 2015.

Shade, Robert J. *Forbes Road.* Sunshine Hill Press, 2012.

About the Author

R. Greg Lau taught high school history for thirty years. He has a bachelor's degree and a master's degree in education. He and his wife, Martha, also had a successful sheep farm and wool business called Country Spun, which was featured in *Colonial Homes* magazine, the *Washington Post*, *USA Today*, and many other publications and television programs. Upon retirement, they also operated a bed and breakfast called Bedford's Covered Bridge Inn for fourteen years, affording them an opportunity to meet people from around the world.

Reading, and now writing, along with church, fly-fishing, gardening, and wood splitting, are among the activities he still pursues.

CPSIA information can be obtained
at www.ICGtesting.com
Printed in the USA
BVHW071405160222
629137BV00001B/84